CHARLIE CHAPLIN'S LAST DANCE

A Novel

FABIO STASSI

*Translated from the Italian
by Stephen Twilley*

BOOKS

Published by Portobello Books 2014

Portobello Books
12 Addison Avenue
London
W11 4QR

Copyright © Fabio Stassi 2012

First published in Italian as *L'ultimo ballo di Charlot*
in 2012 by Sellerio Editore, Palermo, Italy

Translation copyright © Stephen Twilley 2014

The rights of Fabio Stassi to be identified as the author
of this work and of Stephen Twilley to be identified as
its translator have been asserted by them in accordance
with the Copyright, Designs and Patents Act 1988

A CIP catalogue record for this book
is available from the British Library

1 3 5 7 9 10 8 6 4 2

ISBN 978 1 84627 527 2
eISBN 978 1 84627 529 6

www.portobellobooks.com

Typeset in Garamond by Patty Rennie
Printed in the UK by Page Bros Norwich

CHARLIE CHAPLIN'S
LAST DANCE

Born in 1962, FABIO STASSI is regarded as one of Italy's most ambitious and talented writers. He has previously published three novels and has won the Vittorini Prize for best first novel, as well as the Palmi Prize and the Coni Prize. He lives in Viterbo and works in the Oriental Institute Library of the University of Rome. *Charlie Chaplin's Last Dance* was shortlisted for the Campiello Prize and is the first of his novels to be translated into English.

STEPHEN TWILLEY is managing editor of the online review *Public Books* and the translator of *The Story of Maturity* by Francesco Pacifico and *The First True Lie* by Marina Mander. His translation of *The Siren: Stories* by Giuseppe Tomasi di Lampedusa is forthcoming from New York Review Books Classics.

Among his guests was Jascha Heifetz, the celebrated violinist. Everybody was clamorous to have Heifetz play the violin. He picked up Chaplin's violin and started to play and he was astounded, as were the rest of the company, to find nothing but insane dissonance issue from the strings.

Chaplin smiled, took his fiddle from Heifetz's hands and played a bit of Bach with his left hand. All the strings were on backward.

'You see,' said Chaplin, 'I am a being made inside out and upside down. When I turn my back on you in the screen, you are looking at something as expressive as a face. I am back foremost.'

New York Times Book Review and Magazine,

12 December 1920

And there was always someone turning the crank...

The machine sizzled, sounding just like an egg on a stove, the Geneva drive began to rotate, along with the shutter blades, and the film advanced in jerks, like a track cyclist on a curve – slow pedal strokes, sweat, a watchful eye, and at last the plunge...

A sword of light that rent the darkness.

Emerging from a box and expanding gradually, it created two perfect diagonals in the hall. This alone is already a spectacle. You could simply sit there looking, without understanding: smoke and light, and in that light, dust, nothing but dust, tiny suspended particles swimming through the air; they rise and fall, pursue one another, play at imitating the universe... But, if you squinted your eyes and looked closely, inside all that dust you soon saw men with walrus moustaches, a policeman's baton, a dog, a garden hose, an old Ford, cream pies flying, a soda water siphon, workers leaving a factory, a train pulling into a station, and marvellous lighter-than-air women bobbing up and down. You could see a woman's hips in that sword of light, but trying to touch them was useless, you'd never succeed.

It all happened before the light struck an obstacle and everything

I

reformed into images. Before the moustaches were stamped on men's faces, and the women got back to their feet, and the horses pulled away at a canter.

It lasted only as long as it took to get from the projector to the white fabric screen at the other end.

For me cinema was the duration of that journey.

The first few times I didn't even turn my head towards the screen.

The films didn't interest me, just that dust in the air, its movement.

When I finally tell my story, I used to say to myself, that's where I'll start. From the moment the projector's crank starts to turn.

My entire story resides in that space before the screen.

Believe it or not, it's the story of the man who invented cinema before the Lumière brothers or Max Skladanowsky's Bioscop.

A Harlequinade in black and white, for Christmas night.

A romantic pantomime in a world of sawdust, laughter, and tears.

Interior, Night.
24 December 1971

It's Christmas Eve, 1971. An eighty-two-year-old man enters a room and turns on the light. Sunk in an armchair beside the window sits a cloaked figure, Death.

DEATH: I've been waiting for you.

The man wears shapeless, threadbare trousers and a tight-fitting jacket. He tips his bowler hat in greeting.

MAN: As have I. Sixty years ago a fortune teller told me you would come today.

DEATH: Is that why you're in costume?

The man begins, with weary penguin tread, to move about the room. He bumps into a chair leg and begs its pardon. He also apologizes to the rug and to the lamp near the wall.
The figure observes him solemnly.
Then the man stops, takes off his hat.

MAN: I was only trying to make you laugh.

DEATH: Not even a child would laugh at you now. Drop this pathetic farce and let's be on our way.

The man experiences again the panic of his New York debut... He strains to make a silly face, but he feels like crying.

MAN: But my son Christopher is only nine years old. He still needs me. I want to see him grow up a bit more.

DEATH: You should have thought of that before, when you brought him into the world at such an advanced age.

MAN: My wife has always said she married a young man.

DEATH: Well, your wife is very kind...

MAN: It's not fair. I called for you so many times when I was little – as young as my son is now – and we lived in a garret in London, and I'd bang my head every time I went to sit down on the bed, while my mother stared out the window...

DEATH: It was not yet your time.

MAN: I'd cry and repeat my address so you could come and take me: 3 Pownall Terrace, top floor.

DEATH: Enough, it's getting late.

MAN: Wait, not yet, not yet. I'll... I'll make you laugh, it's the only thing I know how to do.

DEATH: No one has ever made me laugh.

MAN: I will, I'm sure of it. Watch this.

The man tries one stunt after another, but in vain. It seems a lifetime since he last performed.

DEATH: You've become a pathetic old man, truly pathetic. Go and get changed. You won't want to come like this.

The man is miserable. His fake moustache becomes detached and falls to the ground. As he stoops to retrieve it his back gives out, halfway down. The man is stuck there, at the centre of a rug, unable to draw himself up: defeated, decrepit, and in pain.

DEATH: Ha!

The man pauses, confused. It sounded as though Death had stifled a laugh, but the pain has blocked up his ears. And yet he is not mistaken: Death is silently laughing, so hard that the man half expected to see tears spring from his eye sockets.

MAN: You're laughing…

DEATH: At you, I'm laughing at you. Just look at the state you're in.

MAN (*unsuccessfully trying to pull himself up*): I thought you said that no one ever made you laugh.

DEATH: Ah, no, you're right, no one…

MAN: No one, except me. So, let me make you a wager (*suffering as he speaks from his uncomfortable position*): You'll leave me now, but come again next Christmas, and if I make you laugh again, you'll let me live another year…

5

DEATH (*intrigued in spite of himself*): Well… Don't think it will be so easy. Tonight I let myself go.

MAN: I'll do my best.

DEATH: I shouldn't be negotiating with an actor.

MAN: It's an honest wager.

DEATH: Agreed then, Tramp, I'll return in a year's time. You've earned that at least.

MAN: Until next Christmas, then.

Death instantly disappears from the armchair. The man hobbles over to lean on the desk and heaves a deep sigh of relief.

FIRST REEL

Dear Christopher James,

This evening will mark my eighty-eighth Christmas. Once again, I will spend it with my family, and the story I am about to tell is my gift to you. I know that I owe you a debt I cannot settle. You're my last child, barely fifteen years old, conceived when I was more than seventy. You will grow up without me. So now I need to hurry, to pass this on to you, before the news of my demise sparks a global uproar. According to what a fortune teller told me in San Francisco back in 1910, I should have already died six Christmases ago, of bronchial pneumonia, after a long life of extraordinary fortune.

Instead, for the past six years, each Christmas, I've received a visit from Death. He sits and waits for me. I put on my vagabond's get-up and perform one of my old sketches for him. As long as I manage to make him laugh, he grants me another year of life. It's our pact. I won't die as long as I continue to amuse him. But I have to admit my act has been looking rustier and rustier these past few years.

I wouldn't have got so much as a smile out of him if it hadn't been for old age itself, the most laughable age of all.

These six years have proved themselves an immense blessing. I wanted to see you grow up, become strong, learn music, and I have. But tonight I feel sure that Death will remain cold and grave, sunk in my armchair, even if I come up with a perfect gag. Because perfection doesn't make people laugh, Christopher. This will be the last time I put on my Tramp costume. I feel it in my bones and my bones have never lied: I am about to shuffle off this stage. But all in all, if I am to go, I don't mind that Death comes for me on a day such as this, when the world celebrates the birth of a child.

I want to devote these last hours to you. There are still so many things we've never spoken about, things that I want you to know.

So, here I am, in full costume, like in the old days. I've put on black eye make-up and once again turned to my box of fake moustaches – if you don't put them on just right, you're a goner.

I write to you from the small boxwood table in the corner of my room. I'm convinced that on small, compact tables, ideas stay together, and you don't have to chase them like geckos across a wall, you just stretch out an arm and take them by the tail.

Everyone knows everything about my life, or just about.

Years ago I published an autobiography that appeared everywhere, and thousands of pages have been written about me by other people, too. My name, simply spoken aloud, elicits recognition, admiration even, in every corner of the planet, from Burma to Tierra del Fuego. Or, perhaps it would be better to say: the name of the character I created, one rainy afternoon in 1914 during the shooting of a short film, by picking out some ill-fitting clothes in a men's wardrobe. I've told this story every which way before, but I'm always surprised to remember the mysterious ease with which the Tramp – or *Charlot*, as many people know him – came into being.

But, for all these words already written about my career, there are some things that I've never told anyone: about how my career in cinema really began, and about how cinema itself really began. These are things that not even your mother, my dearest Oona, would have believed. But I'm old enough at this point not to worry about my reputation or anything else. At my age it's easy to become confused. And anyway, how believable is it to claim to have shaken the hand of Debussy or Stravinsky, of Rubinstein, Brecht, or Gandhi, to have played tennis, in short shorts, with Eisenstein and Buñuel, to have been received by kings, princes and presidents, or that Albert Einstein himself burst into tears like a child when he watched my films? My memory is such a cabinet of wonders that I no longer know if I have really lived what it contains, or if I have dreamed it. For me there can be no clear line between the things that have happened to me and those I've always invented alone in my head. Let me, even, appear a bit ridiculous in my old age: it could only do me good, because contrary to common opinion I've been a terribly serious man, obsessed with perfection.

Of course, there have always been plenty of people ready to bad-mouth me. And now jealous colleagues, or any McCarthyists still left after the shame of Vietnam, can finally hold up my ravings about a more just, free, and humane society as proof of my lunacy. Of course the Nazis hated me as well, despite the fact I didn't have the good fortune to be Jewish. They banned *The Gold Rush*, portrayed me with a hook nose, called me a little Jewish acrobat, loathsome and insufferable in equal measure. It wasn't the first time I was persecuted, nor would it be the last. From the beginning, in Pennsylvania and South Carolina, branches of the Klu Klux Klan and the Evangelical Ministers' Association (scores of good American Christians who sprinkled kerosene on more than just reels of celluloid), had censured and banned my films. But not even the men with swastikas could prevent my little fellow, whose unpolished voice had only been heard previously singing a nonsense song, from climbing onto Europe's most important stage dressed as a barber; no one else had succeeded in stealing the microphone from Hitler… But the moment the Tramp stepped off that stage in 1940, I never could find him again. He was swept away like a dust cloud on the road to Auschwitz or Buchenwald: everything he had to say, he said all at once.

But tonight I'm the one who's going to tell you everything all in one breath, and I'd rather not be interrupted once I get going. Of you I ask just a small effort of imagination, because my story ranges far from the glowing Swiss meadows that surround our home. I had none of the serenity of a mountain lake then, when I was a tramp for real, with no need to play a role.

It's time I told you where I was born. It wasn't in London, like you see written everywhere – even though no one has ever found an official document to back that up – but in a black forest near Smethwick in the English Midlands, inside a street artists' caravan called the Gypsy Queen. It was 1889, the year after Louis Aimé Augustin Le Prince shot the first film short in cinema history: a scene lasting the eternity of two seconds. Since the very beginning, the circus, my life, and the history of cinema have been much more tightly bound up together than anyone could imagine.

As soon as I came into the world, my parents split up. That's just the way things went for me.

As you know, your grandmother Hannah was a soubrette in the variety theatre. She went by the name of Lily, and had a talent for faces. She would stare out of a window and place her hands against the glass as if she were counting someone's heartbeats. She would study people, then imitate them: the way they walked, how they tipped their hats, the expressions they made. But one day something inside her began to crack: she lost sleep, her voice, and her sustenance (ten shillings a week); the light of her beauty dimmed, and she rapidly went to pieces.

Your grandfather was an artist as well: a professional singer, improviser, and storyteller. According to your grandmother he resembled Napoleon Bonaparte, but like many theatre performers he did nothing but drink. I almost never saw him, and when I did I always came away with an unpleasant impression. Alcohol had robbed him of all charm, destroyed his career and his blood. The last time I met him was in a pub on Kennington Road. It was also the first time he'd ever hugged me in his life.

More often, I spent time with my own grandfather, my

mother's father, who repaired shoes in London, in his little house in East Lane. For a while, I cherished the thought of becoming a cobbler like him. It was a trade that fascinated me. I liked the smell of leather and glue, working with one's hands, the patience it required. My grandfather had built a work bench in his kitchen and spent all his time there, even nights. His wife no longer lived with him. After sewing shoe uppers for years, she discovered a taste for younger men and became the black sheep of the family; later she sold used clothes on the street to get by. I saw very little of that vagabond, unfortunately, but it's thanks to her that I know I haven't a single drop of blue blood in my veins.

Luckily I always had Syd, my older brother, with me; without his help I'd never have amounted to anything. Owing to our financial straits, Syd and I spent a couple of winters in a school for orphans and destitute children, on the banks of the Thames. But Syd knew how to instil confidence: when things were rough, he'd grab his trumpet and blow, puffing up his cheeks so comically that all my gloom would melt away. And he knew how to have fun with words, constantly coming up with new tongue-twisters, nonsense rhymes, and memory games for the empty days.

By the age of five I had already made my theatre debut, singing Jack Jones's numbers in place of my mother. She had got stuck halfway through a song and couldn't continue. It was the first sign of her illness. From the audience came a rain of whistles, seat cushions, coins. I knew that song by heart and undeniably pulled it off that day, but it would be too easy now to speak of it as my destiny. The truth is that I gave myself up to the footlights only to save my mother from humiliation and madness. Behind everything I did later on was that angry promise, made by a child full of shame, to become the greatest actor in the world.

After that we moved to Manchester, where I learned how to dance in clogs and joined seven other young boys in a troupe called the Eight Lancashire Lads. People came to see us dance and to have a laugh. Before long, we landed a pantomime gig at the London Hippodrome, in *Cinderella*.

It was Christmas, like now. Eighty years have gone by since then. Eighty long years. And still I remember it better than what I ate yesterday.

That's where I learned how to do somersaults and flips and to walk around on my hands. The Hippodrome had a circus ring that would sometimes be flooded with water to make the stage designs and ballets even more spectacular. They dressed me in a costume with a tail and told me to slink around Cinderella's legs like a cat.

It was there, just outside that ring one evening as I practised my role, that I heard something that changed my life. It was a conversation between the big white clown Marceline and the juggler Zarmo. At the time I barely knew how to read or write, but I knew how to listen. I've never forgotten a word of that dialogue.

'They're calling it the invention of the century, have you seen it?'

Before replying, Zarmo tossed three coloured balls into the air.

'It's the cinematograph, my dear Marceline.'

'Yes, and the cinematograph will send us all packing, you'll see. Who'll still come to the circus or the theatre to see how a mime or a clown moves?'

'Look at it another way: there's no knowing if the cinematograph will succeed, but you can't deny its fascination.'

'You know these two French brothers all the newspapers are talking up so much? If I had the chance I'd strangle them with my own hands. This contraption they've invented: they've no idea what it means.'

'C'mon now, enough. You'll change your tune when the cinematograph becomes an art.'

'It's all pretend, Zarmo, it's a lie.'

'But you yourself pretend to be something you're not, whenever you're onstage. You make people see things that don't exist. Isn't that your job?'

'I'm a mime, Zarmo, and that means taking a personal risk. All of us take risks in our acts. The aerialists, the acrobats, the animal tamers risk their lives. We risk failure: failing to surprise or amuse our audience, failing to make them laugh. We could have a heart attack onstage, out of fear, or forget what we have to do. But we're feeling exactly the same emotion as those watching. We're all living the same life, in the same moment.'

'I imagine the cinematograph has risks of its own.'

'But it's not real life as it takes place, Zarmo. It's an action inscribed on a plate, you can redo it as many times as you like, until it comes off. It's a trick.'

'You're a funny chap, Marceline. I don't understand you. In any case, those French brothers aren't the ones you'd have to strangle…'

'What do you mean?'

16

'I mean: they're not the ones who invented the cinematograph, like everyone's saying. It was one of their countrymen.'

'Who are you talking about?'

'You don't know? I thought everyone round here knew…'

'I don't.'

'Ah, well, it's clear you haven't been paying attention.'

'So tell me then, who was it?'

'Arlequin.'

'Arlequin.'

'That's right.'

'That black-as-night fellow? The one who cleans up after the elephants and pulls the props out of the ring?'

'Yup.'

'But the poor man's an idiot.'

'Do you remember Eszter, the Hungarian horsewoman who was famous for a while a few years back, then completely disappeared from the scene?'

'It's been a while, but who could forget Eszter? She was the most beautiful woman Great Britain had ever seen; everyone fell in love with her.'

'Including Arlequin.'

'Arlequin has been in love?'

'What, do you think he's blind, that he doesn't have a heart?'

'Nobody's ever seen him with a woman…'

'He's never had a girlfriend or a wife, so… what? You think that anyone who's never had a woman before has never been in love?'

'Fine. But, what does all this have to do with the invention of the cinematograph?'

'It matters because Eszter was engaged for an American tour, and Arlequin was afraid of losing her.'

'And how did you come to know this?'

'From Mad Frieda, who was working with us then as the cannonball woman; she heard him crying every night. Once she and Dogface Jo Jo asked him why. "I won't be able to see her any more," Arlequin told them. At first Frieda thought he was talking about his queen elephant or the white Bengal tiger, because the animals were leaving for America too. "You'll see her in your memories, Arlequin," Jo Jo told him. "My memories are as black as I am," Arlequin replied. "So then make a drawing of her." "Drawings don't move," Arlequin insisted. "Ask Mr Bretchley for a photograph." "Photographs are just as still." "So make one that moves." "There's no such thing as a moving photograph." "So invent one," Jo Jo said, winking one of his furry eyes at Frieda. Jo Jo is like that, you never know if he's joking or not, he's always making fun of everyone, and that night he was making fun of Arlequin. Frieda was already regretting being there. The way Arlequin had spoken, his voice so full of sadness, had moved her. She would have liked to lay a hand on his arm, to console him, but she didn't. She moved off with a lump in her throat. But after that, Arlequin stopped crying.'

'Where is this heading, Zarmo?'

'The rest of the story is simple: Arlequin learned to draw.'

'Now you've really lost me.'

'He learned to make drawings that move, I mean.'

'You must be crazy.'

'I'm not crazy, Marceline. Arlequin shut himself up in a cage with his animals, first with a pencil and charcoal and pieces of paper, then with copper plates and glass plates, silver nitrate, gelatine, celluloid, and who knows what other bizarre stuff. He built and dismantled all these strange mechanical devices. Like he was possessed. I don't know how he did it. Word was that not long after he'd arrived from the colonies, before he discovered the circus, he'd followed an itinerant photographer around France. They sold portraits for a few cents at the fairs, along with frames, astrolabes, and magic lanterns, and if need be, they'd recolour the stained-glass windows of churches. It was a rumour, perhaps, but I heard it from more than one source. "You can tell that he was born in a camera obscura," Jo Jo said, when he learned this story. "He must have been exposed to too much light, heh heh…" But nobody laughed at that nonsense. The truth is that no one knows what his experiments amounted to, except the tigers and the elephants. Arlequin told Hans, the dwarf, that he was training himself not to forget. The evening before Eszter's departure he was ready. He hid among the feet of the spectators at the edge of the ring, with a wooden box propped up on his legs, and waited for her appearance…'

'And…'

'And with this crank-operated box he took a photograph, my dear Marceline, but not just any photograph; the photo-graph he took was something alive.'

'You seriously expect me to believe that that idiot Arlequin…'

'Yes, Marceline, he captured everything, even the blood pulsing beneath her skin.'

'That's impossible.'

'If you'd put your eye to the box, you too would have been

swept off your feet, believe me, and you would have felt your stomach turn, because everything inside that box was upside down and in movement – the horses, the ring, the lights – and in the midst of that whirlwind Eszter alone kept her balance... Of course, Mr Bretchley, our manager, never knew about it, otherwise he would have made it his circus's main act: Come, ladies and gentlemen, come one and all, to see the Thief of Time, the only man capable of stealing your soul, and then showing it to you!'

'And why didn't anyone tell him about it?'

'Who would ever have believed that this extraordinary invention came from a lowly circus drudge, someone who cleans up after the animals? A photograph that moves! Bah, even you don't believe it, and you're one of us. Arlequin couldn't read or write.'

'But he could have shown his magic box to someone...'

'He showed it to us, we're his family, but he wasn't interested in making it public or in filling the Thames with pound notes. He did it just for Eszter, so he could keep seeing her dance after she left.'

'I'd have liked to see that myself. Did she ever come back to London?'

'No, after the accident she never returned. Her career finished there.'

'What a sad affair.'

'Maybe it was fate: no sooner has Europe's greatest dancer arrived in America than she falls from a horse.'

'There's never been another one like her...'

'So, do you believe me, then?'

'Is there any proof?'

'I heard that when part of the company left for a new tour, Arlequin entrusted his invention to Hans. He told him, "It's the gift I didn't give her the day everyone said goodbye. Go to America and make sure she gets it, it belongs to her." But no one ever heard anything more about it, not about Hans, or the box, or Eszter.'

'A strange tale.'

'It certainly is.'

'One last thing, Zarmo, why do they call him Arlequin?'

'The name was given to him many years ago, as a joke, by an Italian who worked with us. "*Ehi, Arlecchino*," he said once, "*vieni qua*, come here." Everyone thought it was funny since the Harlequin costume can have all the colours of the rainbow, but not black. So that became his name, and we used the French version: Arlequin.'

So there you have it: that's what I heard that day. Word for word. From two of the greatest performers I've ever known. Your jaw would have dropped to see Zarmo at work. For instance, when he used to balance a billiard cue on his chin and toss a pair of balls on top – he was so good you always had the impression that the cue was about to fall. 'It took me years to learn how to mess up,' he said. Marceline, on the other hand, was a marvellous mime – an art that the cinematograph really did kill, much later. He taught me everything that can be done with a bamboo cane, and how expressive a face can be without pulling faces, or even moving your head. In *Cinderella* I had to make him fall off a chair, and during rehearsals I put so much energy into it he nearly broke a leg. He picked himself up off the ground and slowly brushed the

21

dust from his knees, but instead of scolding me, he burst out laughing. He carried on laughing as he retrieved his fishing rod and stepped back up onto the stool. I remember him like that: in the centre of the ring, attempting, with diamonds as bait, to fish out the chorus girls swimming in the flooded ring. He wore a long-tailed coat, a bow tie above a white waistcoat – white like his cheeks – and a straw hat whose rim he would carefully stroke. He never said a word onstage, and yet he had the most beautiful and gentle voice you'd ever heard. One evening he sat down next to me and told me that his real name was Isidro Marcelino Orbes Casanova. I asked him how he became a clown. 'When I was seven I fell asleep in a lion's cage,' he said, winking, 'and when I woke up I was too far from Zaragoza and my family to go back. To get hired I did seven flips in front of the Barcelonès circus director.'

I know that these stories seem ancient and perhaps worthless now, but that Christmas, Marceline was the toast of London, just as he would be later in New York. For a while his star burned every bit as bright as that of the illusionist Harry Houdini. But even though Marceline was capable of jumping over eight men lined up in a row, and imitating all manner of emotions while remaining absolutely still, he was always a timid acrobat, disoriented by life. The last time I saw him, towards the very end of his career, he had signed on to be one of the countless clowns running through the three rings of the Ringling Brothers circus. This was after an accident, the success of the cinema, and two failed restaurants had reduced him to poverty. That evening, I entered the dressing room, where I found him slowly removing his make-up. He seemed like a sad, lethargic old animal, unable to lift even a single paw. He didn't wait for Death to come and find him, but shot himself in a shabby New York artists' boarding house, the Mansfield, on Fiftieth Street...

At the time I overheard that conversation between Zarmo and Marceline, I had no idea what they were talking about. I was just a lad of eight years, and yet, I was struck by the story of Arlequin.

I'd occasionally seen him before, but he was one of those types who passed through life without making a sound, and he was so black that if some night, after he'd finished cleaning up the arena, he'd crossed the ground in the nude, nobody would have seen him. Now I wanted to speak to him myself.

It was the secret training hour: trapezes flew, jugglers' clubs and rings rose skyward, and clowns pulled faces as they circled the ring on absurdly tall or short bicycles. Right in front of my nose passed a fifteen-foot giraffe with its drooping neck, blue tongue, and two tiny horns on its head.

Coming towards me in a striped costume was a woman broader than a zinc washtub. She made you want to push her from one side and then the other, to see if a mammal of those dimensions could be tipped over. This was Frieda, the cannonball woman. She was playing one of Cinderella's stepsisters. Goodness knows how big a cannon mouth had to be to fling her in the air.

'What are you hunting, Pussy Cat?' she asked, casually waving a hand before my eyes.

Her index finger was wider than a house sparrow, and she had some dried purple glue stuck to the nail. But what surprised me was her voice, so thin that if I'd been blind I would have imagined one of those frail girls with no appetite who wander around all alone, with long hair, large, hollow eyes, and a shadow of melancholy in their skinny legs.

'Nothing,' I meowed, 'just stretching my legs.' Frieda burst out laughing.

I made my way towards the animal area. I stumbled twice against the same iron tie beam, declined to respond to a ventriloquist, and ran into a dancing bear holding hands with its master.

'Pardon me, sir, do you know where I can find the negro Arlequin?' I asked a man in a striped suit, waistcoat, and gloves, carrying a cane, ready for the ball.

'Kid, your voice has more cracks than my ribs, what's the problem?'

I stared at his thin, grey goatee, at the wings of woolly hair over his ears. Even fully clothed, he was the skinniest man I had ever seen: it looked as if, under his trousers, there were just two wooden sticks. He extended his hand warmly and I clasped it, but the bones of his fingers gave an alarming squeak. The man began to laugh.

'No need to be afraid, it's a joke I play on everyone. I'm the human skeleton here. My name's Jack, like all the skeletons in England. And you? You're not exactly built like a colossus.'

His laughter seemed false and out of place to me.

'If you're looking for Arlequin, you'll find him down that way. It was a pleasure to meet you.'

But before I could take my leave, a figure jumped from one of the caravans, wearing a long red dressing gown belted tightly above the waist. A threatening abundance of hair came down over his eyes and around his nose, covering his cheeks, ears, and nostrils, invading his jaws and forehead. All that was still human about him were his pupils and lips. And his smooth, white hands.

'What are you looking at, dwarf?'

Mysteriously, that man with the face of a beast spoke my language.

'You should see him in a jacket and tie,' said the human skeleton as he walked away with an unsteady, zigzagging gait. 'Jo Jo is the handsomest Prince Charming the world's ever seen.'

I watched them disappear together under a tier of seats.

The crack of a whip let me know that I had finally arrived at the animal cages. Suddenly, my heart began to leap up my throat like a bird ruffling its feathers. Mr Bretchley, the impresario of *Cinderella at the Circus* – so ran the title on the posters covering London at the time – looked me up and down. He removed a cigar from his mouth as he took in my feline costume.

'Hmm, a tough case,' he said, slowly chewing over each syllable, the better to retain the tobacco flavour. 'At first glance, I'd say you were a half-portion. I can't put you in the bearded pygmies number, because you're too tall, but you won't fit into Ruben the Magician's act either. Sorry, son, but you're going to have to make do with playing the cat for a bit longer.'

Mr Bretchley wasn't the type to drag things out. He finished saying his piece and went back to smoking.

I finally found Arlequin emptying a bucket. He turned slightly. A strange light rained down, and across his face there passed the shadow of a trapeze that was moving above him in the breeze. His hands were both covered with dirt. The trapeze swung back and a smile rose upon Arlequin's face at seeing me. He sat down on the edge of the ring, in front of a row of empty seats.

That's how I remember him, as he wiped away the damp earth that had stuck to his fingers. I don't know how to explain it, but suddenly I was sure – like only an eight-year-old can be – that once upon a time his hands too had known how to draw the eyes of an audience, juggling rings, clubs, and torches, even if now they seemed only to convey his own melancholy.

You learn an awful lot from cleaning out animal cages. For instance: to remove elephant dung you need hemp sacks at least a yard wide, and with camel dung you can build a house. Arlequin's hands – those same hands that first invented the cinematograph – knew that with soil it was impossible to separate anything out: peat from manure, dust from ashes, the wet from the dry. Everything is the same fertile earth, the same bare sand. Even silence, which is full of words, and time, made up of memories like roots sunk deep. I had wanted to ask Arlequin about his invention, and about Eszter, but that night, as a young boy in the face of Arlequin's expressive silence, all my questions fell silent too…

But perhaps all this reminiscence sounds as tedious and worthless as an old out-of-tune pianola? If I carry on like this, Death will certainly take me away this very evening. And yet, for me memories have always been, more than anything else, a matter of hands.

26

Let me explain. Once Mr Bretchley told us how, when he worked for the Bastiani brothers, he had signed up a dwarf with no arms. On account of injuries suffered in the war. Or malaria. Or perhaps he was born that way. They called him Goliath. And it seemed like a joke, but Goliath's teeth possessed superhuman strength. If you put a bit in his mouth like they do with horses, Goliath could drag a caravan full of giraffes, with clowns on top, and monkeys too. The act was always a hit. The trouble was that one day Goliath got lost. The circus was set up outside Saint Petersburg, overlooking a river delta. Goliath said he wanted to see what a country full of snow was like; he went out and never came back. Bretchley railed at the poachers. At the tundra wolves. At the anarchist terrorists. The truth was much simpler. Goliath was not able to find the grounds again because he always forgot everything. He had even forgotten the cause of his own dismemberment. And this forgetfulness wasn't caused by the bursting of blood vessels in his temples as he clenched his jaws, but because he no longer had a single hand to hold on to his past with, or to save himself from sinking in the snow.

Three years later my father was given an indigent burial, in Tooting Cemetery; my mother was committed to a lunatic asylum for good; and I took up running.

That was how the new century began for me. Miles and miles at a run.

My brother Syd had enlisted in the Navy, but I wanted to become England's greatest runner: Charlie the marathon man. I trained for months, pushing my physical endurance to the limit. I won a twenty-five-pound prize in Nottingham on a twenty-mile course, and a few years later only a bad cough kept me from participating in the London Olympics.

For money, in those years, I used to sell gillyflowers outside the Kennington Road pubs and was apprenticed to an Andalusian barber with a shop on Chester Street. He claimed to have shaved Robert Louis Stevenson once. When we had no customers, he would pull a guitar out of a closet and begin to play flamenco, his great passion. He would explain to me how the music was composed of a *canto grande*, a *canto profundo*, and a *canto mínimo*, like all things, and how it brought him *duende*, a kind of sadness that inflames the blood. It wasn't clear what he was trying to say, but I felt like I understood him, as if there had also been a Spanish musician or two in the gypsy caravan where I was born. My job at the barber's was to lather up people's faces. You wouldn't believe how different one is from another – coarse, angular, or plump... it came naturally to me to imitate them in the mirror as I massaged their cheeks – I couldn't help it. Those waiting their turn would catch sight of me in the mirror over the current customer's shoulders and soon the entire shop would burst into laughter. In a matter of days the touchier clients had had me sent packing.

A little later I lost another job, as a major-domo, for having built a long horn instrument out of a downspout in my spare time. They said I was slacking. In my defence I said that I'd always loved music, but they fired me all the same. So I began making simple toys and selling them at fairs on behalf of two Scotsmen, until I finally got a break. Blackmore's theatrical agency landed me the part of a newspaper hawker

– which I performed with considerable realism – in a comedy prophetically titled *From Rags to Riches*. Immediately after that – when I must have been around your age – they gave me the role of the pageboy Billy in *Sherlock Holmes*.

But the trouble continued. The moment I got my first wages, I went off and bought a box camera. No one knew where to track me down and I turned up late to a matinée performance in front of 2,000 people. When I got to the dressing room my understudy was already in costume and ready to go on. A flood of sorrow coursed through me, so powerful that it ruptured some capillaries in my nose. A red-headed actress quickly pushed me into the women's dressing room, and it was those actresses, all older than me and half naked, who stopped my nosebleed, who stripped me and dressed me in such a cheerful and energetic hurry that they succeeded in getting me onstage in time for my cue. I don't know, but perhaps it is due to that improvised rescue that female nudity has always given me a sense of irrepressible euphoria and enthusiasm…

Anyway, it was not long after my brother's return from the Navy that I finally took my place in the great circus that was Fred Karno's company, the Fun Factory, for three pounds a week. When Karno met me for the first time, I failed to utter a single word. He thought I was too shy and sad and sulky for the theatre, and if it hadn't been for Syd, who had already started working for him, Fred Karno never would have given me a shot. At first he said I could work as a mime, not as an actor, but with a couple of trials I invented so many imaginary languages and absurd accents that he changed his mind for good about my voice. Within a few weeks he was consulting me on every number, and soon I was feeding him good ideas for his routines.

There was only one player who was better than me, even though he was still learning the ropes. He was a skinny boy with a bumbling manner, straight-straight hair, and eyes always on the point of tears. At the time he still used his own name, Arthur Stanley Jefferson, but everyone would come to know him as Stan Laurel.

I was with Stan when I first came to America, for a tour in 1909. But things didn't happen quite the way I've always said they did, with the ship hugging the Canadian coast, passing the island of Newfoundland, sailing up the Saint Lawrence River and docking in Quebec City one foggy and rainy day.

No, I've kept the real story of that voyage – and why it came about – to myself. The truth, the only truth, was that I had just fallen in love, in London, with a fifteen-year-old girl. She had hair the colour of young red wine, a waist thinner than an amphora's neck, and she seemed like the best dancer I had ever known. In reality she was just a second-rate show-girl, but I'd happened to see her once as she was changing in the wings. I nearly slipped and fell right then and there, and her fellow dancers laughed. She planted her amused brown eyes on me, and I looked at her lips, and her legs, and I introduced myself. 'Charlie Chaplin,' I said awkwardly. 'Hetty Kelly,' she said. For the next two weeks I was incapable of eradicating her from my mind, like a clinging vine.

You'll see how it happens, the first time it happens to you: you can't breathe, you toss and turn in bed at night without sleeping, you start to do all kinds of foolish things. I attempted to cut my sufferings short and asked her to marry me on our first date. I've never been shy with women. As I said, I've grown up in the promiscuous atmosphere of the theatre, surrounded by the bodies of hundreds of actresses and singers undressing together between one number and the next, and I've never felt any embarrassment whatsoever. But Hetty's lips, and her smile, they made me blush. I took her out to dinner at the Trocadero, near Piccadilly Circus, but it wasn't a great night. Our affair lasted a kiss and eleven days. Fred Karno must have picked up on my state of mind because the following week he sent me away from London: first to Paris, to the Folies-Bergère, and then on a steamship called *Kangaroo* bound for New York, along with gaunt-faced Stan. 'You two have become a couple of hotheads,' he said as he gave us the tickets, 'but there's still time to give up on the theatre. The trip will do you good.' We were the two most promising players in his stable and he wanted us really to get the hang of what the Americans called *vaudeville* and the French, improbably enough, *music-hall*. If we didn't get lost on the way, he said he'd bet his hat we'd become excellent actors.

In Karno's shoes I wouldn't have risked a single pound on my name. In Paris I was struck mute once again. I'd see myself reflected in the shop windows of Montmartre, insignificant and spindly like a coat stand. I was sure I wouldn't be able to cross any ocean without that girl. So the night we left for the United States, I tried to flee. But Karno had thought of everything. He'd stuck me with a Spanish dwarf who called himself *Mosca*, the fly, and he never let me out of his sight. Technically, Hetty didn't ever give me an answer to my proposal; she just sent word that she'd never really taken it seriously. Yet for me this wasn't the joke of some insolent, penniless mummer. The truth is that, as far as love goes, I have remained an eternal novice, and it was only your mother who partially cured me of my rash behaviour. *America*, in any case, was a word that sounded both sweet and poisonous to my ears: my father had done his own tour in New York, shortly after my birth, but that trip was ultimately responsible for the break-up of his marriage and the beginning of his decline.

From the moment I stepped onto that steamship I never stopped crying. I cried tearlessly, and as soon as we set sail I was overcome by nausea and cramps. After two days I looked like a dead man. I spent the entire voyage in the hold on a straw mattress. Mosca slept at my feet. It was hardly comfortable, but at least down below I couldn't see the sea.

It was a terrible journey. It took three weeks to reach the mouth of the Hudson River; between trouble with the boilers and bad weather, we spent countless extra hours stuck in the middle of the Atlantic. Three weeks of nausea and convulsions in which the passengers on the *Kangaroo* did nothing but vomit over the side of the vessel, with such violence that it brought on hiccups, as if they were trying to rid themselves of a store of tiny stones hidden at their temples, or beneath their toenails, or shut up in their lung sacs. And afterwards, they were alone, with their empty stomachs and green tongues, while the ocean swept away their past existence. Pale, with swollen eyes rolling back in their heads, they saw their former lives bobbing on the water, a wake of rotting white flowers that spread and slowly slipped into the deep. Those who suffered worst were the old folks and the women. Little by little, the sea dried up their skin and their words alike: they didn't even have a name for the last gobbet of sorrow that persisted inside them and couldn't be spat out. The children, on the other hand, became accustomed to the sea in no time. They were sick for a few days but then quickly invented new games, excited by the voyage and by the novelty of daily life on board.

At some point or other, then, everyone was sick. Except for me: I kept everything in my mouth. I was bent over double with cramps, but I didn't want to forget anything. I didn't want to forget Hetty Kelly's legs in the hallway of a theatre – I never would have succeeded – and I didn't want to forget who I was, and the place I came from, the asylum where my mother was held, and the words I'd heard spoken by Zarmo and Marceline years before. I struggled against myself. Angrily, I chewed up everything I'd seen of the world so far and drove it back down.

Whenever we stopped in the middle of the Atlantic, with the motors turned off and with no wind, the *Kangaroo* seemed like a bird resting on the water, and I felt happy. Those breaks revived my hope that it was still possible to reverse our route and suspend destiny. But in the end, the turbines would start up again with iron obstinacy, never going fast enough for us to travel more than 200 miles in a day. As soon as we were on the move, I'd hurry to hole myself up again in the cargo hold, before another attack of irrational panic spread through my body and brought on a fever.

The *Kangaroo* distributed goods and collected the desperate.

Neither the travel conditions nor the trip's duration could ever be mistaken for those of a pleasure cruise, but for the price it suited everyone just fine.

The doctor who examined us every week had said: 'Keep your eyes wide open, otherwise you won't make it into America.' And he'd explained how a few years earlier New York had opened new immigrant inspection stations. They had already acquired many names: The Island of Tears, the Penal Colony, the Customs House... Great heaps of grey stone, sometimes taking up entire islands. 'As soon as you disembark,' he told us, 'the first thing they'll check will be your vision; if you caught an eye disease on the ship, you'll be sent back. The scientific term for it is trachoma.'

On these crossings, not even cholera inspired such terror.

'They also send away freaks of nature,' the doctor had added, 'deaf mutes and idiots. They chalk an X on their backs and hustle them back aboard the ships they came in on, along with any pregnant women.'

But Mosca, Stan, and I never passed through one of those stations. No boat came to ferry us over, unlike some other poor devils, who threw themselves into the sea and were fished out below the Statue of Liberty. Notwithstanding all our permits and letters of presentation, Mosca was convinced they wouldn't let in a dwarf like him. Nor Stan, because, just to look at him, no one would ever have imagined he was so intelligent. But if they'd heard him speak... He'd dish up one quip after another, at a dizzying pace, and if you stopped to listen to him for even a minute you'd feel seasick all over again. And indeed he was the one who came up with a plan on that occasion, while I persisted in a scheme of my own:

to guarantee that they'd send me back, I made sure to keep my eyes closed, even at the risk of falling overboard or of bumping into all the corners on the ship and covering myself in bruises.

At night I dreamed that all the children on the ship followed my example and began to stumble about the ship with me, forcing the captain to run up a flag signalling danger, as if the ship had some wretched, ragged plague on board, and couldn't drop anchor in any port. In my dream the ship had to leave again immediately, to abandon these waters and return its cargo of blind boys to their homes, to no longer poison their blood or their eyes nor push them to make their future somewhere else just because that's the way the world works.

With my eyes closed I squeezed past wave after wave of rising bodies as I descended one by one the steps that led to the hold. There are times, even now, when I still dream of being there, groping my way down the inside corridor of a steamship and repeating my oath to give me strength as I stand before the dark, dirty stairs that are used only for taking down empty bottles and rubbish. A woman grabs me by the arm and drags me along with her. She places my arms against a railing and tells me to hold on tight. No one is paying attention to us any more. Then the *Kangaroo* sends forth an elephant's trumpet, and the madness of all that uprooted humanity, desperate to play its ticket in the lottery of life, surges back up from the holds, through the body of the ship, making the handrails and metal deck plates vibrate, pulling me along...

*

As we approached New York Bay, I screwed up my eyes tight to keep out every last sliver of light. I was twenty years old and America was more than four hundred. The wind sprayed saltwater in the faces of the passengers assembled on deck to gaze over the railings at the New World, and my life was about to change for ever. To celebrate our arrival, the crew even brought out the stowaways and the emigrant families, and in the melee, one of the sailors lifted me onto his shoulders and carried me up into the fresh air. He put me down facing the wrong way, with my back to the land.

So, while the rest of the ship was looking at New York, I was still staring at the ocean.

And this is the last thing I remember from the first part of my life: an expanse of water that flooded my eyes and prevented me from breathing. According to the calendar, the month of November 1909 was just two days old, and it was there, on a half-rusty steamer with the blue line of the horizon before me, that I made my decision and uttered my vow.

America: I would not so much as look at it.

That day, the wind of the New World struck me in the face at exactly the same moment that another object struck my head.

It was Mosca, with the toe of one of his reinforced boots. Stan had ordered him to do it. I hit the deck. Together Mosca and Stan carried me into a side room and dumped me into a grand piano, where they also hid themselves. As the steamship was being tied up at a New York City pier or off who knows what island of tears, I passed the time in the darkness of the piano creating a nonsense rhyme in my head, like a puppet in a whale. I set about listing all the black things I knew. A piece of volcanic rock given to me by my brother. My grandmother's dress. Tar stains on the soles of my feet, which could only be removed with pumice stone. A line of ants on the granite countertop. A priest's cassock. A cockroach that had climbed up onto my thigh, in London, under a table. The boats on the Thames. The trousers of the old men in Covent Garden. Blackberries on a bush...

And before unloading had begun, I was done.

Black like obsidian,

Black like pitch,

Black like a rain cloud,

Black like a billiard ball,

Black like the pirate flag and the gown of a priest,

Black like smoke, mud, coal,

Black like ink,

Black like a boot,

Black like... America. This was the first colour America had for me.

Thanks to the stratagem of an actor as thin as copper wire and a dwarf's ankle boot, I arrived in America in a piano. It was set down on solid ground, in the land of Freedom, along with a cargo of instruments bound for a small theatre. No one asked for our documents or X'd our backs. Our entrance into the New Continent was truly a musical one.

You want to know my first impression of New York? They set us down in the back of this theatre and left us there. The familiar smell of backstage and the boards, at night, drew us out, like mice catching a whiff of home. I've always found it irresistible, something that takes you back to childhood. I remember a pale gleam of light coming down from a skylight, weakly illuminating the hall, all those empty seats. I took a few steps centre stage and promptly forgot Hetty, London, my oath – everything.

I found myself immersed in a new solitude, full of promise. So it is that, each time you're reborn in life, you have to learn how to raise yourself, to never stop being reborn. The consciousness of being a different person, of being else-where, filled me with joy. I would keep my eyes wide open, that much was certain; I would try to see everything, even the back of things. I would fill every theatre in which I happened to perform. I would conquer that city.

In a corner I found a violin, tossed aside along with its battered black case. It must have been damaged in transit. It lay there, curled up like a dog that's been beaten by his master. I picked it up as we made our way out into the street.

A mild night greeted us. It may have been November but it felt like summer. The lights of New York, the people rushing by, in noisy groups or alone, the irreverence of the skyscrapers, the glare of the electric signs, the old men on benches staring at their feet, the drunks looking for a doorstep or fire escape to sleep on – it was all part of the same atmosphere of madness, a show that was being put on just for me and that was showing me life for what it was, in its splendour and its horror, and little in between.

Our troupe had a deal to work in some fellow's theatre chain, a six-week gig, and we showed up on time at the appointment arranged for us by Fred Karno. If things had gone well, we would have crossed the United States from coast to coast, through the drugstores of the Midwest, the hog farms, the gloomy haze of Chicago and its most famous brothel, the House of All Nations, where prostitutes from every country could have proclaimed me King of All Refugees and Emigrants... We would have performed alongside a comedy troupe from Montana, descending the bony shoulder blades of America until finally being blessed by California, by its fields of oranges, its shameless quantities of light.

But things didn't go well; things didn't go well at all. Our debut was a colossal fiasco. My first joke was greeted with glacial silence, and I was terror-stricken. American audiences were very different from English ones. I didn't make anyone laugh. Our sketches seemed weak and repetitive. This is exactly what I'd been afraid would happen; I'd tried to warn the promoters and the other actors, during rehearsals, but everyone, apart from Stan, had dismissed me as a gloomy, sullen killjoy who never drank and only thought about putting aside the money he made. The performance finished to general indifference, which is even worse than being booed. I felt the same panic I'd seen in my mother's eyes when her voice cracked during the Jack Jones song. A good portion of the audience had already left the theatre before the show was over, without so much as a backwards glance. All my expectations crumbled. I'd spent my whole life building up the confidence necessary to go onstage; it took me a single evening to lose it. I thought I'd never be able to step onto the boards again. At least, not for a long time.

Stan and I had rented a basement room in a sandstone

building on Forty-third Street, next to a laundry that sent forth the steamy stench of dirty clothes. The sound of the laundresses coughing came through our windows and kept me awake. In the two weeks leading up to our disastrous debut, Stan and I had practised day and night in that room, like when we played hockey for Karno's team, obsessively going over everything each of us had ever learned. I taught him how to round a corner at a full run, skip-hopping on one leg and rotating the body on its axis, extending the other leg out sideways for balance. It was a move I'd seen done in London by a variety actor called Will Murray and I'd liked it right away. But most of the time I sat down and watched. What kind of barman do you have in your head, I'd ask him in that bleach-smelling basement behind Times Square, who mixes all these ideas for you? Stan squeezed his cheeks and raised a hand: to my surprise, a small flame burned at the tip of his thumb. I never did figure out what kind of magic that was, otherwise I'd have used it too, I swear. But the trick was unrepeatable because Stan's own body gave off small electric charges like a piece of amber. I used to worry he would set the building on fire just by walking around the room.

One evening Stan had come home with his eyes brighter than two flash-lamps. I was cooking an egg. He took the pan from my hand and flipped the egg high in the air. 'Charlie,' he said, 'I've come up with a new character.' The egg fell back into the centre of the pan, breaking to pieces. 'He's a poor boy, like you were, and completely defenceless, but as soon as he falls asleep he imagines himself defeating every peril, he's invincible. I'll call him Jimmy the Fearless, what do you think?' He lowered his head and when he raised it again he seemed like a ballet dancer dancing down a chalk line between reality and dreams, with a lightness I'd never observed in any acrobat. As it happens he was, in the most elegant way possible, throwing back in my face a part that I had stolen from him in London after an opening night. I was proud of it as one is proud of a gift; for once, I was his stand-in. He was the best, and the most generous. Even though Stan had only performed the role in public for one evening, the soul of his Jimmy went straight into the Tramp, when the time came. But Stan's greatest coup was to convince the world that he was stupid, as if he was permanently stuck in some corner of his adolescence. To this day, I regret not having made even a single picture with him, especially once he'd dropped out of circulation and people had stopped offering him work. But the United States of America had already revoked my re-entry permit, old age for some of us seemed like an insult, and besides, seeing Stan made me ashamed for all I had stolen from him…

Anyway, not even Stan could give me back the confidence I'd lost out there on a Manhattan stage. The day after our appalling debut I took out a shirt, put it in my bag along with a pair of holey socks and a toothbrush, and picked up my ruined violin. I left Stan a note, wishing him all the good fortune someone with his sensitivity and talent deserved. I'd seen him on the hockey rink, seen the powerful hits his ostensibly frail frame was capable of, and how he would fly on his rusty skates. I was sure he'd know exactly how to talk his way out of this one. To Mosca I wrote that I wouldn't get him into trouble with Fred Karno — I would return for the end of the tour or after a few months. I was heading out alone to study the world and to seek my destiny, if destiny existed, somewhere out there. In order to become the actor I wanted to be, I had to learn how to get inside people's heads, to get by on my own, to watch. I had to make sure every movement was born of observation from life. There are no short cuts. If I wanted to be believable, I had to recreate in fiction what I had lived in fact. The tricks I knew no longer worked on this side of the ocean.

That was the day I became the Tramp, *Charlot*, the vagabond with the bowler hat and bamboo cane, and not in a movie studio three or four years later. The American tour I made then in my shabby clothes was no caper from theatre to theatre, as I always let people believe, but a long, solitary voyage among people who got by on their wits or didn't get by at all, in the heart of a dazed, eccentric, and miserable humanity. The life led by other actors, distant from everything, concentrated exclusively on their profession, didn't interest me. In a few months I learned a good many other trades beyond those I'd already picked up in London, and became acquainted with an indefinite number of situations and characters. You could say I was storing up ideas for use during the rest of my career. My skin took on more colours than a cuttlefish or a chameleon. It was a second apprenticeship, this time as a twenty-year-old, and it perfectly complemented the one I had undertaken in childhood.

Before cinema crossed my path – or I its, I still haven't determined which – I considered raising hogs and making sausages. Taking advantage of my size, I worked as a jockey at a pair of hippodromes in Texas and New Mexico. I picked tulips during daylight hours, and, by night, boxed in a dozen or so gyms across the Southern states, a difficult but profitable venture: they paid me to take punches throughout the match and only go down in the last round.

I followed a strict diet, travelled by train, and kept myself clean, especially my teeth, so I would always be proud to laugh, even if I often fell prey to irrational outbursts of anger and melancholy. In any free time, I would play the violin. I'd repaired the soundboard with a bit of cobbler's glue similar to the kind my grandfather once used and, since I'm left-handed, I'd mounted the strings in reverse. In every city I visited I'd steal a secret or two from the local musicians and reproduce it on my instrument. When the opportunity arose – but only ever on my last night in a city – I would allow myself to play cards.

My goal was California.

In Las Vegas I tried to sell multipurpose vacuum cleaners that transformed into blenders, my own patented design. I always introduced myself in the same way, with the biggest and boldest smile I knew: 'Hello,' I'd say, 'my name is Charlie and I've got an idea that will make you rich.' Only two German immigrants, each with one squinty and one normal eye, owners of a small household-appliance company, offered to mass-produce my prototype. I'm still convinced that if they'd actually done it my name would have for ever taken the place of that of William Hoover, the vacuum king…

And after that came the strangest period – and at this point it seems strange even to me – when I worked as an embalmer, a boxing trainer, and a typographer. I've never told anyone about this.

Interior, Night.
24 December 1972

Death sits in an armchair.

The Tramp careens from one side of the room to the other, as if walking a ship deck on the high seas. He lifts one foot, about to fall. He brings his hands to his bowler hat. He has the face of someone who hasn't eaten for days. He tries to set the table but fails. Somehow, he manages to reach the desk and sit down. He rests a cheek on one hand in a dreamy pose. He imagines himself surrounded by a group of disreputable women. He stands and bows, as if preparing to make a speech. A declaration of love. But his only interlocutor is the figure before him. He quickly sits back down.

Then, taking up a fork in each hand, he spears two bread rolls from a basket. He brings them up nearly to his chin and begins to raise and lower them as if they were his legs and an orchestra was playing for him. He swings them through the air. From one side, then the other. He wheels them around in circles. But his fingers, deformed by arthritis, struggle to grip the forks. The movements of his hands are heavy, graceless. Like the steps of a ballerina who has forgotten her part and whose muscles are so far gone she's always on the point of falling.

The Tramp bends forward. His face is grave. He concludes the bread roll number with the slowest, most exhausted of splits.

DEATH: If you think you can make me laugh with these old tricks…

The Tramp doesn't move; the rolls stay split.

CHARLIE: Once I could even imitate Nijinsky and Pavlova.

DEATH: Once… Come now, at least put on a decent suit.

CHARLIE: Why? I can't come like this?

DEATH: It wouldn't be suitable.

CHARLIE: One has to dress for dinner in the other world?

DEATH: No, that's not it.

CHARLIE: What is it, then? I'd have worn this same outfit even to testify before the House Un-American Activities Committee, just as if I'd been invited to a reunion of old comedians. But it wasn't necessary for me to be there to end up under investigation and sent into exile…

DEATH: Senator McCarthy was right: you are an incurable communist.

CHARLIE: I'm sick of hearing people tell me what side I'm on.

DEATH: I am not people.

CHARLIE: And I'm an internationalist, not a communist.

DEATH: Internationalist, pacifist, anarchist, utopian… it's all the same.

CHARLIE: But don't you see what a bunch of lonely

45

islands we've become? Of mass murderers...

DEATH: You're still all the same handful of earth.

CHARLIE: I can't believe it, even *you've* become bourgeois! You who always were the last one to make distinctions on the basis of race, faith, membership in one club or another...

DEATH: Me?

CHARLIE: You, yes, you, the greatest internationalist of them all, more Marxist than Rosa Luxemburg or Antonio Gramsci...

DEATH: I've never become involved in politics...

CHARLIE: That's because, like me, you're only interested in mankind.

DEATH (*rising*): Fine, then, come as you please, even in those rags if it makes you happy, just be quiet.

CHARLIE: It's already been a year?

DEATH: You got what you wanted. Now stand up, it's time.

CHARLIE: I can't.

DEATH: Don't start again about your son.

CHARLIE: It's not about my son.

DEATH: So let's go, then.

CHARLIE: I can't, I'm stuck.

DEATH: Enough moaning, enough excuses. You're not funny any more, so get a move on.

The Tramp attempts to rise, pushing down with his arms on the table, but he's a frozen frame. Death throws his hands up in the air, drops them to his thighs, then takes his seat again. The Tramp continues to press down with his wrists but to no avail. He touches

46

his nose with a bread roll... Death drums his skeletal fingers on the chair arm.

CHARLIE (*in an irritated voice*): Well, are you going to do
              your job? Are you coming to take me away or
              not?
DEATH: This is ridiculous...

Death approaches him from behind, takes hold beneath his arms, and pulls.

DEATH: And one, and two, and... three.
CHARLIE: Come on, come on then, coooome on.

The Tramp's face has gone purple and Death is breathing hard; nonetheless he plants his feet and tries to hoist Charlie up.
    Crack!

DEATH: Oooouch!
CHARLIE: What are you doing? Why have you stopped
              pulling?
DEATH: My back.
CHARLIE: What?

Stunned, the Tramp stares into Death's cowl. No words emerge from the blackness, just a moan. The Tramp's cheeks swell like a trumpet player's. From his throat slowly rises a cough that he tries to stifle but that finally explodes into a guffaw, to which Death succumbs, and together they both nearly split their sides laughing.

DEATH: Why, you've done it again, you old fox. Ha ha
          ha!

And then, along with his laughter, Death disappears.

The Tramp finally stands, clutching his belly, and tries to make for the hallway. But his feet can only move so fast.

SECOND REEL

It was on the road to Santa Cruz that I met a fellow with a shaggy blond goatee at the centre of a smooth face, like a stand of stubbly straw in the middle of a meadow. His name was Anthony Deeds and he had a sweet shop in Watsonville. He suggested that I travel around the nearby towns and sell the candies he made. I accepted because I no longer had anything to lose, and because I could not afford to turn down any offer of work. But in the course of three days I had just one child hold out his pennies, take his colourful packet, and hurry away. The problem was me: I looked sadder than a scarecrow. Doctor Deeds understood, and from that day on he had me put on an apron and work in the shop.

In actual fact, we sold more candy to old folks than to children. At certain hours of the day they would fill the shop like flocks of migratory birds resting on the branches of a tree, and while I weighed out a quarter or a half pound of sweets they would sit off to one side and peck at their memories for entire afternoons. There was Mr Pierre, who had a lovely toothless smile, like Casanova in retirement; I used to write rhyming verses for him behind the counter to send in greeting cards to the ladies in town. And there was Mrs Dixie, a landlady and a bigot ever more convinced that one of her tenants, an unemployed man who never paid rent, intended to poison her with sambuca and then cremate her in the kitchen oven. And Mr McKay, a former gold-digger who always talked about a mine he lost in his youth. Sometimes I'd also see an old alcoholic actor who now worked as a dormitory watchman. I would give everyone some liquorice or a jelly bean, sometimes a little boat made out of newspaper.

It wasn't a bad life. You heard all kinds of stories; they came and went just like the sweets, one after the other. But before long, impatience had returned to tickle my feet and one morning I couldn't take it any more. I took off my apron and hung it on a wooden hook, penned a rhyming couplet for Mr Deeds, pulled on my hat, and finally hit the road again for Santa Cruz.

Essentially my lot was none other than that of an orphan out for a stroll in America, an orphan unsure if he was still seeking his Shangri-La or had already lost it. Before arriving in Santa Cruz, I stopped for some hours to look at Monterey Bay. It reminded me of the water of the Thames, thousands of miles away.

I reached Santa Cruz at sunset. My first impression was of a city of houses painted white, as fishermen's houses always are, which the evening sky had water-coloured red. The men who filled the streets cast long shadows against the walls. Even I cast a long shadow: no one would have believed it belonged to such a short man, and I observed it with pride as I walked. This was how, on the following day, I ran bang into Archibald Lawster. His enormous crooked nose was the first part of his body I encountered.

'For the love of God, boy, have you got your eyes in your ears?' shouted Mr Archibald when he managed to speak.

I was afraid I'd broken his nose because my head stung with pain. A straight right from Jack Johnson, the most famous boxer of the day, couldn't have hurt more. Stunned, I remained on the ground for a few minutes. It was Mr Archibald himself who pulled me up. He had briefly smoothed his overcoat; otherwise he didn't appear to have been troubled.

'I believe you could do with a glass of water,' he said, and hauled me across the street and into his store. As I entered I thought I glimpsed a squirrel in the window, but Archibald Lawster was already pushing over a chair and sitting me down. Once my breathing and heart rate returned to normal, I was finally able to look around and discovered that I was surrounded by animals of all kinds: pythons, wolfhounds, moose, boars, mouflons with curling horns, ducks, and Siamese cats. On the floor, one shadow longer than the others extended all the way to the threshold. I turned and to my shame caught my breath in an uncontrollable, unseemly gulp. A six-foot bear with upraised arms and an open mouth stared furiously down at me.

'No need to be afraid,' said Mr Archibald just as I was about to throw myself through the door. 'That's Juan Perez, my wife's grandfather. I called him that even when my wife was alive. She'd always get offended and her eyes would go all big and red, and I'd say to her, "Whoa, now you can really see the resemblance!"'

I continued to tremble.

'The bear's stuffed, my boy: relax. Getting him here was no mean feat. The hunter who sold him to me walked away with plenty in his pocket, I assure you. But Juan Perez is my masterpiece. I sweated over him for four years, and in the end I think I managed to preserve him in the best way possible. Even a pharaoh of ancient Egypt would be satisfied. Folks who don't know him are always startled at first: I've lost a lot of customers that way.'

'What exactly do you do?' I asked, still in a daze.

'I'm an embalmer, my boy. There are loads of people who ask me to stuff their beloved animal who died, others who would rather have a dead one from the beginning, so they buy themselves a dog, say, or a beaver or a parakeet, for the home. They say it keeps them company. At first I didn't understand, but now I've ended up alone too, I often find myself talking to Juan Perez, or just staring into his eyes, which are made of glass, actually.'

I drank down in a single gulp the glass of water Mr Archibald had brought me – and a firestorm flared in my stomach. Mr Archibald wasted no time in delivering two hearty slaps to my back.

'There you are, my boy, fixed up and in peace with the animal world.'

'What the devil did you give me to drink?' I asked as soon as I got my voice back.

'Rum, my boy. The same thing the filibusters off our coast drank two hundred years ago. Pour a single drop down the throat of Juan Perez, and five seconds later we'd have a drunk bear stumbling around the shop.'

And that was how I made the acquaintance of Archibald Lawster. Thanks to my shadow, the desiccated carcass of a bear, and a bottle of pirate rum.

I stayed two months in that shop. Mr Archibald had told me he needed an assistant, because at that point he felt too tired to continue the work on his own, and if Heaven had brought us together – had us literally run into each other – there had to be a reason. It was his wife who had led me to him, he was certain. I just think that talking to Juan Perez was no longer enough for him.

'I'll teach you the trade,' he promised me.

I didn't have to think twice – I'd liked the fellow right away – but I never did learn the trade. It's not easy to capture the personality of an animal in an eternal mask. I skinned lots of carcasses, emptied their veins, pulled out intestines and nerves, sewed up mouths, handled the formalin and every type of unguent and resin.

But to achieve the desired final result required talent I did not possess. You must have hands as steady as a surgeon's, and lots of patience. And even this isn't enough to restore the cheerful lightness that a sea lion can have as he sits up on a rock. What's needed is a kind of divination. You have to isolate a single gesture among billions of gestures, a single pose, a single habitual move. I stuffed a fair number of birds, snakes, ants, fish, but they always ended up with their eyes crossed or with the wrong attitude: a seal with the gaze of a lynx, frogs who give the impression of moving like snails. I did nothing but eternalize grimaces. My only triumph came in the form of a small band of shrew mice that I had arranged together and placed in the shop window, where they attracted all the children in the neighbourhood. My dream was one day to embalm an elephant, a polar bear, or a horse.

'Once I tried to immortalize a woman,' said Mr Archibald one morning, out of the blue, as we grappled with a particularly well-feathered owl.

'I was young and ambitious, but it wasn't for the money. I was thrilled by the possibility of challenging Death all the way. Being a nimbler thief than the greatest thief there is. Spiriting away from him a human being, a face... A gangster from San Francisco asked me to do it. They'd killed his fiancée a week before the wedding and he wanted to preserve her in a glass case for the rest of his life. The police poured into his house before I could finish and it was lucky they did. I wasn't yet ready for a job like that – it would have been a disaster. I got off with a brief vacation in Folsom prison. And, to tell you the truth, my boy, my time there wasn't so bad. The other inmates respected me; so did the guards and the warden. They were frightened by my nickname: the Taxidermist. I discovered that all kinds of tall tales were being told about me, all over the penitentiary. Even the worst inmates, the Red Shirts, the ones who make it their business to welcome the newcomers, left me in peace. It's down to a lucky mistake, but Folsom really was a harmless stretch...'

Absorbed in his thoughts, Archibald Lawster was using a small brush to wet the owl's head. I watched him for a few minutes.

'You never tried again, after that?' I finally asked because I couldn't stand the silence, but I regretted my curiosity immediately.

'The madness returned two years ago, Charlie, when my wife died,' he responded gently. 'Finally, I had all the experience necessary to fix a woman's body and skin for good. But any single expression would have cancelled all the others. And I wanted to preserve them all. I wanted to remember the face she had when she was young, when she'd watch me from behind a fan, hiding her freckles. Or the morning we went up to a roof terrace and she sat down in a way that was all her own, sinking slowly at the centre of a white chenille dressing gown trimmed with brightly coloured flowers. I even wanted to remember the fear in her eyes during her illness, and the day she conquered all fear, venturing the first steps of a waltz in the middle of the room before taking definitively to bed. No, there must be another way to embalm our memories, one that allows them still to move.'

He slowly opened the wings of the owl, as if he held a puppet in his hands, then Mr Archibald stood and went out to the street to smoke.

I continued to work with him for a little while yet, but eventually the loneliness proved contagious. When I realized I was becoming as introverted and melancholy as Juan Perez, I decided the time had come to set out once more. With a pencil I sketched the exaggerated profile of Mr Archibald's nose on a sheet of paper and under that I wrote:

If there's a way to embalm memory, sir, I will find it.

It was a promise.
I thought it would please him. And I meant it, too.

*

Out of work, I slept in the Cathedral of St Joseph for a time, but then I got myself hired on a trial basis in a glazier's workshop. I was keen to drum up trade. On the street I'd met a young lad with his cap pulled low, his hands in his pockets, and a sly look in his eyes. I asked him what he did. 'I'm a conjurer,' he replied, 'I work in a world of deceit.' I suddenly recalled an old trick I'd learned from Fred Karno, who had worked as a glassman before becoming an impresario. I offered this lad, Jackie, a penny for each day his sling picked out a window. He accepted, but the very next week we were caught by a guard whose moustache had one end up and one down, and I had to leave the glazier's to avoid bigger trouble.

Immediately after that I found work in a candle factory. My task was to insert a lead core inside the wick, to keep it upright, limiting the risk of fires. I found myself more at ease with candles than I'd been with dead animals. At that point I had a certain familiarity with resins and mineral oils, but in the factory I also learned how to handle beeswax, soy wax, tallow, and that strange white and pearly substance called paraffin. Here they produced candles of every kind and soon I was able to recognize the different lights that each flame could provide.

At the time I was renting a room from an old man with even wilder ideas than my father's. His name was Martin Sycomore and he lived in a fairly run-down, multiply mortgaged cottage, together with a handful of nephews and nieces. He offered me a room on the ground floor at a price that seemed entirely too low, and I accepted immediately, fearing he would retract the offer. It didn't take me long to figure out why he'd named such a modest figure: each member of the family played a musical instrument and they practised at the oddest hours. On some days – or, more precisely, some nights – it seemed like I was living in a musical conservatory. From the kitchen came the high-pitched whistle of a clarinet; from the dining room, the bichords of a viola; and from the first room off the hall, the nightingale song of a transverse flute and the more substantial sound that emerged from the pistons of a bass tuba, a shiny parade instrument so long and heavy that it could only be played sitting down. I quickly adapted to the situation, enthusiastically adding my violin to the symphony. There I could play whenever I wanted, for as long as I wanted, without fear of disturbing anyone.

The house was strewn with personalities beyond those in the amateur orchestra. You might also come across Uncle Boris, always fussing with black powders and metal mortars, who as soon as night fell would go hunting will-o'-the-wisps with a butterfly net; or Aunt Peggy, who wrote cloak-and-dagger novels; or Cousin Paul, who was a stamp collector. But the person who filled me with irrational, heedless cheer in those weeks was Alice, a niece studying dance and Russian, as luminously beautiful as a sunflower. I'm not the type to draw things out, so just let me say: Alice and I became involved. It started in one of that hovel's closets, and then up against the bark of a big white hickory tree. I wanted to know what an American's lips were like, and Alice taught me. For a few weeks we took never-ending Sunday walks in the Los Santos forest. Her enthusiasm always took me by surprise. I would transform a loaf of bread into an accordion, a musician's trick for making it last longer that distracted us from our hunger and made Alice laugh until she cried. But she could be happy about anything. I thought I might carry on living with her in that curious house for the rest of my life.

You see, Alice was the first girl who ever fell asleep at my side. She would serenely press her hips back into mine, then allow herself to drift off to sleep, giving herself entirely over to my care, and I would cease to breathe, because it's so rare to become a refuge for someone, even if only for a few minutes or hours.

Early one evening, we stopped at a viewing point to look out over San Francisco Bay. The colour of the ocean changed constantly. First blue, then bright green, finally dark green. Two barges were pulled up on the beach. I made out the name of the one painted red: *Harborless Voyager*. Beyond there was a long strip of land, lights twinkling.

'I hope I will meet a man with your hands,' Alice said.

Crashing waves drowned out her voice.

The next morning it was my turn to find a goodbye note under the pillow. One with neither verses nor drawings, however. With just a plea for forgiveness.

After all, someone has to support my family
and pay the mortgage...
The world will be emptier, without you.

This time Alice had preceded me. She'd hopped a train to find work in Canada and I'd never see her again. But I instantly forgave her. Strangely, I realized that the little bit of happiness she'd given me was enough.

The day after she left, I too said goodbye to old Sycomore

and all his relatives, embracing them one by one, in silence. Then, without looking back, I hit the road, but I wasn't sad. Behind me, a clarinet intoned the adagio from the concerto in A major, K.622, by Wolfgang Amadeus Mozart.

Many years later, I spent a long, simultaneously happy and melancholy evening in the company of a director – originally from Italy, he was even shorter than me, and someone I cared for very much – in which we challenged each other to recount our enduring illusions and our young loves. I remembered Alice then. I don't think he believed me, but he enjoyed the story all the same. 'It's a wonderful idea for a movie,' he said. We'd played cards for it, and I lost.

'San Francisco is a new city,' the barman told me in the first place I stopped for an ice-cold beer. 'If you've got ambitions for your life, boy, this is the right place for you.'

It wasn't the first time someone had said that to me, but I'd already been travelling around America for some time by now, and here I was, still sitting on a barstool.

'It's been less than four years since the earthquake,' the barman continued, 'and we've rebuilt it from the ground up, as God is my witness. Between the shaking and the fires, everything came down: the mansions in Nob Hill and the shacks down by the port, the theatres, the Opera, the omnibus... Market Street became Inferno Avenue. Mountains of rubble on every side, advertising billboards on the ground, twisted metal towers stripped of their walls, facades of burned-out buildings with nothing behind their windows... and right in the middle of it, all those men scurrying from place to place, all the bicycles and waggons. Men repairing the tracks, men headed to the homeless shelter where they fed everyone at big tables outside. You can see it with your own eyes, if you like: there's a handful of work sites still open. The rest of the city has nearly returned to how it was, though; even better than it was, if you ask me.'

I planted my elbows on the bar and observed the teeming street. The man was right: hustle and bustle were stirring up clouds, not just of dust but of dollars. San Francisco would get me back on my feet, I could feel it. If the city had risen again, after an earthquake and a fire of those proportions, enough to set the whole world talking, well, why shouldn't I believe I'd make it as well?

At the end of Market Street I came across a curtained shop window that drew my attention. A sign there read:

YOUR FORTUNE TOLD BY HANDS AND CARDS
— ONE DOLLAR

I stood there awhile. Fine, I thought, saving a dollar won't make me rich anyway. I pushed aside the curtain of strung shells and went in. The lights were tinged red. A woman ordered me to sit down at a small table. 'Take this deck of cards, shuffle it three times, and then show me your palms,' she said brusquely. She had fleshy cheeks and was chewing something, a chunk of meat, maybe. Behind her on a shelf, I counted ten small bottles containing a strange green unguent. Her table was covered with candles and empty tortoise shells and from somewhere emanated the smell of incense and other essential oils. No sooner had I opened my hands than the woman nearly choked on what she was eating. 'I have never seen a hand like yours,' she said. 'You will find incredible success and make a vast fortune.' I thought that she was making fun of me and I stood up from my chair. 'You'll find your way soon enough, kid,' the woman went on, 'and it will be an extraordinary way.' I was suddenly angry. I started to shout, saying that some people might happily pay even more than a dollar to hear this kind of nonsense, but that wasn't the case with me. I didn't want to be deluded by anyone, and especially not by a miserable soothsayer like her. I turned my back and hurried away, but not before I heard her final prediction, like a curse: 'You will die at Christmas,' said the woman as I exited her establishment, 'at the age of eighty-two, of bronchial pneumonia.' The echo of her voice has been with me all my life, especially during these last six years, but it won't be long now before part of her prophecy really comes to pass.

The encounter shook me up. It seemed like I no longer knew my place in the world. As I walked down Third Street, accompanied by a pack of dark thoughts, I was suddenly set upon by an odour that I knew well, of sweat and damp towels. It came from an entrance below street level, in the middle of a new block of grey on grey flats. It hit me like a slap in the face, and I couldn't resist the temptation to go and meet it. I descended the few steps from the pavement, then another interior staircase. At the bottom, the unmistakable din of a boxing gym set my blood racing. It's incredible, the amount of noise produced by a human being dancing on his toes and pounding a swinging bag or the muscles of an opponent, moving the air with his own breath. A universe of muffled blows that nonetheless rumble through the space, where voices are only good for simple exclamations of encouragement or abuse from the edge of the ring.

I went into the owner's office and told him I needed a refuge, but only for a little while. If he would help me out, I could do anything he wanted, from cleaning up to taking punches. I'd been a boxer who could endure a lot of punishment, who could boast of having been knocked out twenty times (per contract, in the last round).

'If you're looking for a church, you've come to the wrong place. I'm no priest and I don't take in the needy,' replied Webster Duncan in his hoarse smoker's voice.

'I'm much more at home in a gym than in a church, sir,' I said. 'That's why I came here.'

Webster Duncan's face was tired and unshaven. Gripping his jaw in one hand, he stroked his cheek.

'How long's it been since you slept?'

'It's not easy to sleep on an empty stomach. In the last three days I've had nothing but a bowl of soup.'

'You're not putting me on, are you?'

'No, sir, so far I've only told you the truth.'

'Okay, then, let's make a deal: I'll have someone bring you a plate of beef and cabbage and I'll let you sleep in the locker room for tonight. Then tomorrow you clean yourself up and be on your way, agreed?'

'Agreed,' I said, feeling a lump rise in my throat, and I said no more.

A month went by before I set foot outside that gym. Webster took me on as a factotum, and once he saw me at work in some lightweight shoes and heavy gloves, he decided I had a good deal to teach his boys.

The most promising athlete I found there was a sixteen-year-old with a barely visible goatee and a pale, brooding face. They called him Stutters Grogan because his speech defect made it tough for him to finish a sentence. His physique was completely ill-suited to boxing: short arms, a narrow torso, and legs more liable to crumble than bread sticks. But when he punched with his right, you could count the swollen veins on his thin neck. And behind his closed fists, a cold gaze withered your bones, as if he had been assailed by a sudden sadness and now all this sadness was set to erupt from his body with uncontainable fury.

He had a weakness for house sparrows. I don't know how he managed to capture them: with breadcrumbs, I guess. When he came into the gym, he was always carrying some in his pockets, caressing them with his thumbs. He reluctantly turned them over to Webster before training. He would open his big hands, two warm beasts, and inside would be nestling these little birds, their necks broken, like abandoned marionettes.

The first time he came towards me in the ring with his guard raised, I thought: he could win bouts with his eyes alone. An irrational fear spread through my arms, and even after all this time I still can't explain it, but Stutters Grogan would make you aware of all your limits and of where you found yourself in that moment, of the little you had succeeded at in life up till that point and of the nothing you would manage to accomplish afterwards.

And your courage would melt, irrecoverably, away. It's a gift only very few boxers have. The impetus that sends them dancing around the canvas is different from the music that moves everyone else. It's not a matter of money, nor excessive self-regard, as it is for many champions. The feeling is hard to put a name to; it's a drive that comes from deep down and has less to do with victory than with defeat. Grogan's type is as rare as an azalea in a poppy field. The public always picks out such types to fall in love with, because it sees their fragility before it sees their strength, and every time they win the public feels like it's witnessed a miracle, a rebellion against the natural order of things. It's like that with comedians as well. But in the long run, and they themselves are the first to admit it, the fragility that shaped them inevitably gets the better of them, too.

Training them isn't easy. You have to pay extremely close attention, and the normal rules don't apply. It's a matter of teaching them to take care of themselves. This was my job, at least for several weeks. To teach Stutters Grogan to defend himself, above all from his own despair.

I imposed discipline on myself too: I ate only wholewheat bread, slept as much as my body needed, and kept my muscles active. For the first time in my life I had to be a role model for someone else. But my rogue's tricks would never have worked for long, even on the least experienced among the gym's raw young men.

Webster Duncan appreciated my work all the same, because he was a good man and had the eyes of a lamb. Sometimes he would emerge from his office to observe us. I forced our champion to box on sand, wearing a pair of clogs, and I showed him all the moves I had learned with the Eight Lancashire Lads, a treasure trove of feints that would have disoriented any opponent. I amused myself by hiding behind him and copying his steps. I whirled my arms, I clung to him from behind, I surprised him with blows. The other athletes would stop what they were doing and burst out laughing. I wanted to make him leap, like the syllables of the insults that hiccupped in his mouth without finding their way out. Nobody that came after him knew how to dance around a ring like that, and you had to wait for Cassius Clay to see anything similar. A real sand dancer. 'You certainly have some original methods,' Webster would comment as he examined the range of Grogan's bobs and weaves.

When necessary I could even be underhanded. Before anyone else could do it, I ruined his profile with an unannounced uppercut and then sent him to cry in front of a mirror. It's what I wanted: for him to spit out his too young and delicate soul in a locker-room sink and return to the gym more naked and wrinkled than a newborn. 'Never allow the sun of your anger to set on your horizon,' I'd tell him, 'your rage is a gift.'

For days on end, I wore him out with the jump rope and shoulder feints, sent him running through the neighbourhood. Soon he began to resemble a real boxer, with a pronounced depression in the bridge of his nose and prominent cheekbones. After three weeks, we had reached a good point and Stutters Grogan was nearly ready for the blessing of the bell, as they say in boxing circles. Just a few outstanding details remained.

Exactly a month from the day I first entered the gym, Webster and I took our young hopeful to see an exhibition match with Jack Johnson. He was the most famous son of slaves on the planet: a negro who admired Napoleon

Bonaparte and loved Italian opera, who had that summer, in the fifteenth round in front of twenty thousand people, defeated the milky-white ex-champ James J. Jeffries in Reno, Nevada. Boxing, too, in its own way, was a circus of outsized creatures. In fact, the six-foot six-inch cowboy who finally took the world champion title from Johnson some years later finished his own career in Buffalo Bill's Wild West show...

But that evening it seemed like all of San Francisco had come to pay homage to the Galveston Giant. Stutters Grogan had sat down between Webster and me. I could feel his legs shaking against mine; the same thing would sometimes happen to me before I went on stage. He seemed to have a fever. Even a two-syllable word was too much for him to get out. 'You're going to have to get used to it, if you want to do this job,' Webster told him. 'Next time it'll be your skin under the floodlights.' Grogan didn't respond; his eyes became two tiny wet dots. I found the sight of his suffering unbearable. What would I have done if it had been him sitting in the corner of the ring? Would I have thrust him towards his destiny with the same confidence with which I was training him? And how could I be sure that that really was his destiny? These questions weren't just for him. I suddenly needed to stand up. I quickly got to my feet and apologized to the two couples sitting on the bench next to me. In the stairwell leading to the lower tiers of seats, I noticed throngs of men fussing with their wallets in the dark corners. I knew what they were doing – taking bets, on the opening bouts or on the round number in which Johnson would unleash his legendary left. I didn't have to think about it for even a minute. I pulled

68

out the wages that Webster Duncan had given me that morning for my services and staked my wager on the seventh. 'Seventh round,' I said, carefully enunciating the syllables into the ear of a bloke with shiny shoes and an Italian-made chalk-striped suit. 'Johnson will knock him flat in the seventh round.'

The man took my money and recorded the bet in his notebook. I went back and sat down next to Grogan, who continued to sweat for no reason, and waited for the end of the fights between the younger boxers who were just out to get seen.

Finally, following a few absorbing exchanges of blows between a Spaniard and a Canadian, it was Johnson's turn. The crowd greeted him with a roar of applause. The circumference of his arms and legs was staggering. Johnson held out his hands toward the spectators, clasped the gloves of his opponent, a Californian from Sacramento named O'Sullivan, and waited for the referee, a short man in white shirt, bow tie, and long trousers, to give the signal to start.

His style was unmistakable: Johnson would skip about on his toes, his guard low, then suddenly dive into action; his opponent would have no choice but to try to bring his body closer to Johnson's to slow down the crushing mass of flesh launched against him. All the money they'd given him aside, to stick it out up there took guts. In the seventh round beads of sweat formed on the negro's shiny head and, moving with unforeseeable speed, he landed a straight left smack in the middle of the Californian's face that knocked him flat. Earlier I'd figured that this kind of match is never over too quickly, so as not to disappoint the spectators, nor goes on too long, so as not to tire the champion. The seventh round had seemed like a good compromise. I wasn't wrong. O'Sullivan tried to get up and throw himself at Johnson's hips, only to be rocked back by another volley of punches, and this time he sank down on the canvas without a struggle. While he was still on his knees, Johnson caught him with another hook to show everyone that no agreement had been made between them and that in the ring you don't leave any job half-finished. O'Sullivan flopped sideways and landed literally hanging from the bottom rope, with one arm dangling over. The referee went over to the negro and raised up his gloves before he could go back to hitting.

Stutters Grogan was pale. He remained seated as the entire arena rose to their feet. I took advantage of the hub-bub to get away. As I descended the stairs I felt Webster Duncan's eyes on my back. I located the man who had taken my bet and picked up the money owed me. Then I left by a side exit, without returning to my companions. That evening I'd been lucky, but I'd never be able to be a good role model for anyone. Stutters Grogan would make it without me, just like Stan would. Grogan had talent and Webster knew it; Webster was a shrewd man and in a position to help him. Better for me to get out of the way, before I recklessly ruined someone else's hands besides my own. I quickened my step in the direction of downtown San Francisco, in search of a hotel, clutching in my pocket the big bills I'd won and swearing to myself that I would never again set foot in a boxing ring.

*

A few days later I read the following notice in a shop window:

Print Shop Seeks Apprentice
12 Doolittle Avenue
Ask for Willie

Doolittle Avenue was a sloping boulevard with a row of trees running down the centre in the shape of a tuning fork. All the buildings were faced with dark sandstone. At the sight of them I was stung by an attack of nostalgia for the old streets of London, so narrow and different from American streets. Nostalgia is always a treacherous sentiment: it will hide behind an old fire escape and trip you up as it pleases. It would be a perfect comedian's stooge, if it were possible to know its lines in advance.

The door with number 12 on it was white and from behind it came a muffled, rhythmic metallic clanking. As soon as I entered, the noise became so loud that to ask for Willie I had almost to scream. Standing before a pedal-operated machine was a boy who pointed me towards the back of the shop. Willie was an ugly brute of a man with hairy arms and black gloves; the sleeves of his checked shirt had been rolled up to his elbows.

'I saw your ad,' I said. 'I'd like to know if the job's still available and what it is exactly.'

'Any bees in your bonnet?'

'All flown away, sir. At this point I can boast a completely bee-free bonnet.'

'That's fine, good to hear it. So far I've seen nothing but odd ducks in here, students with their smooth white hands and fancy language, or else old bags with puffy powdered cheeks and no idea how to fill their days.'

'I'm just looking for a job.'

'Let's have a look at you.' He looked. 'Well, you've got the right build for it. If you don't make a mess of things I can teach you what you need to do.'

I don't know why, but Willie put me in a good mood that morning, maybe because he made things simple.

'The job pays the same as all the others,' he said, 'not a dollar less and not a dollar more. We don't make distinctions here – everyone works in the same way. And I don't care if you don't know the first thing about this business. It's easy to get you started. There's just one thing I need to know from you: how much patience have you got?'

'Whatever it takes.'

'Would you be capable of sitting for hours on quite an uncomfortable chair?'

'I've done worse.'

He seemed satisfied.

'Right, then. In that closet you'll find some coveralls that'll fit you perfectly. Slip them on and come with me. There's a whole grammar that needs inking.'

The coveralls were grey and stained and not exactly my size, but they would do. I put them on and followed Willie into his shop.

The first thing I learned was to grind up the ink, to get rid of all the lumps and make it smooth like oil. After a week my fingernails were trimmed in black and I had to spend hours every evening cleaning them with cotton balls dipped in acetone. I even got ink on the fingerboard of my violin. But

I felt calmer than I ever had before. The work granted me a tranquillity the likes of which I'd never known.

In addition to ink, I soon became acquainted with that other dense and bituminous substance called petroleum, whose value men so overestimate. In print shops, it's the kerosene used to clean the rollers, dirty water that's carried around in buckets and then dumped down the drain. I had to do it myself at the end of each day, but even this task didn't bother me. I restored shine to the stamps and the lead type of the plates with the greatest care, as if it were a matter of life and death, as if it were my duty to return the alphabet to humanity and erase all the words printed in a day, to be able to start all over anew the next morning.

The print shop run by Willie Cook (to give the man his full name) produced mostly educational materials – text-books, spellers, prosody manuals – but also a few weekly papers and great numbers of popular novels in inexpensive editions.

When Willie decided I was ready he called me in.

'At your age,' he said, 'I apprenticed in one of the most prestigious printing houses in San Francisco. We received plenty of important commissions, even from Europe, and we worked with the embassies. We toiled day and night and never let up.'

Willie gesticulated with his black gloves as he spoke.

'Now I'm going to show you something.'

Slowly he pulled at the tip of his left little finger.

As he finished removing the first glove I saw that the hand that emerged was missing two fingers.

'Allow me to introduce you to Don Quixote and Moll

Flanders, Charlie. My gloves have special stuffing that makes up for the digits I lack, but these are their true faces. You can also call them Molly and Don, if you like. Don is my Ring Finger de la Mancha. He lost one of his phalanges in battle as I was pressing an edition of Cervantes' novel for the royal printing house of Spain, but as you can see he has preserved his gaunt and noble appearance. In the case of Molly, she owes her shape to a vertical press from which I was pulling the last pages of that old thief and pirate Daniel Defoe's book. What once was a typically ungraceful thumb, like more or less everyone's, is now a fleshy lump with wide, sensuous hips, don't you think?'

A shiver ran down my back, the same shiver that comes over me whenever I witness a display of human madness. Yet I couldn't pull my eyes away from that vision because Willie held the hand open before my face like a trophy.

'Not that this kind of thing happens all the time,' he went on, 'there's no need to be frightened, but dealing with books can be much more dangerous than you might think. You notice that everyone wears gloves here. And they don't do it just to keep the ink off. They do it to hide the wounds that books have inflicted on them. The truth is, Charlie, the thousands and thousands of pages I've printed have shaped my body more than my soul, and this is something a printer well knows, better than anyone else.'

With resignation I continued to listen to his raving.

'Even in the best-case scenario, this work leaves invisible signs that radically change you. Now, are you sure you want to go ahead with this apprenticeship?'

Willie Cook had inspired in me a certain amount of anxiety,

but I forced myself to respond with the greatest resolution.

'I'm sure. I want to learn everything there is to learn.'

'All right, Charlie, that's enough with the menial chores, then. I want to put you to the test.'

'Tell me what I have to do…'

'I'm moving you on to composition. But I've still got to choose the book you'll work on, which is important. I would've liked to give you something of particular value, but this isn't a prestigious printing house like the one I worked in when I was young. I can only give you one of our cheap novels. It'll have to be one by either Theodore Dreiser, or Mark Twain, or else Jules Verne. Any preference?'

'What's the title of the Verne?'

'*The Mysterious Island.*'

'And do you know what it's about?'

'From what I've read, it's about an island in the Pacific and a group of castaways, one who's an engineer who invents all kinds of stuff to survive…'

'I'll start with that one, Boss.'

The corner of Willie Cook's mouth twitched with a smile.

'I'll take you to the desk where you'll be working from now on.'

I followed him, curious, little suspecting I wouldn't be getting up from that desk for months. Willie led me to the shop's quietest corner, where he invited me to sit down at a table with a wooden case divided into many compartments, all containing tiny lead bars.

'Stick your fingers in,' he said.

I silently obeyed and felt the faces of the letters tickle my fingertips.

'You've got everything you need here. Consonants on this side, numbers in the central column. Vowels are on the right, down low, while capital letters are higher up, along with the special characters and accents. All you've got to do is keep one hand on the line to fill and fish out the letters with the other.'

Willie showed me the movements I'd need to make. I watched him in some bewilderment.

'It takes a great dose of patience, as I told you. You just have to get used to it. I'll check back in a bit and you tell me how it affects you. Here's the text you'll be composing. Good luck, Charlie.'

Willie placed an old edition of Verne's novel on my desk and walked away. I opened the book and began to read and to work. The first line I composed was a title: *Shipwrecked in the Air*. Forty minutes for just four words. But by lunchtime I'd begun to get the hang of it and by the end of the day I'd completed an entire page.

CHAPTER I. The Hurricane of 1865. Cries in the Air. A Balloon Caught By a Waterspout. The Torn Casing. Only the Sea in Sight...

With great effort Cyrus Smith, the book's protagonist, began to speak by the end of the afternoon. At this rate, I calculated, it would take me a year and a half to complete the task Willie had set me, because *The Mysterious Island* was over five hundred pages long.

'Lightning quick you are not,' Mr Cook said, 'but you didn't give up today, and that's already something.'

That night I collapsed on my bed, every muscle screaming, as if I'd done nothing all day but run, and instead I hadn't once left my seat.

Things went a bit better the next day, and even better the day after that. After a week I matched the speed of the most experienced compositors, and after two I was steaming along like a Union Pacific train. I finished Verne in forty days, sharing in more and more of Cyrus Smith's inventions and coming close to tears as I prepared Captain Nemo's funeral.

I'd acquired a taste for it. I managed to concentrate without effort and no longer experienced any kind of fatigue. Willie was satisfied as well and watched me from the back of the shop with obvious pride. The truth was that I liked the work, and that scoundrel of a printer had had me figured out from the beginning.

After roaming the length and breadth of America I had finally found an occupation that forced me to remain still in one place, with my feet firmly planted on the ground, and what's more, obliged me to read – you could even say I learned how to read in that print shop. It hadn't been so long ago that my brother Syd had had to read aloud for me the lines I was to recite in *Sherlock Holmes*, dividing each word into its component syllables there in our garret. At Willie's, I devoted myself above all to novels. They were a luxury I'd rarely been able to permit myself. But from the first line I composed with my own fingers, I understood that it wasn't simply a matter of reading. I clutched the words in my fists, I could weigh them, measure them, scratch up my skin with them: before they were anything else, for me they were lead, tin, antimony. From that moment and for the rest of my life, I would treat them as a juggler does his objects, always looking to show them in the best light.

Yes, it was much more than reading: I took books apart and put them back together again; I may as well have been rewriting them. I could say that in the time I spent in Willie's shop I recreated some masterpieces of world literature in their entirety, letter for letter, word for word, comma for comma. Willie encouraged my enthusiasm and entrusted me with a series of low-cost fiction titles he printed for a popular publishing house, small volumes with simple, lightweight covers. The first time I saw *The Mysterious Island* bound and ready to be put out for sale I experienced the pride of an author for his own book or a carpenter for a well-made table. For several days I kept going into a bookstore in downtown San Francisco to watch the book from afar, waiting for someone to come in and ask for it.

After Verne I worked on Rudyard Kipling's *Captains Courageous* and *The Man Who Would Be King*, then on Dickens's *A Christmas Carol*, one of Mark Twain's travelogues… in a few months I had read more books than in my entire life to date. I became so good at it I even began to assist the other typographers. I was always the first to finish, so I'd have them pass me a few pages from one of the other volumes in progress. In no particular order, a long series of characters passed through my hands: Gargantua, the lawyer Vidriera, Captain Singleton, Gulliver, Tristram Shandy, Werther, Baron Munchhausen, Oliver Twist, Colonel Chabert, Pechorin, Fabrizio del Dongo, Ahab, Sissy Jupe, Emma Bovary, Pierre Bezukhov, Raskolnikov, Anna Karenina, Huckleberry Finn, Kurt, Buck…

I stayed late to finish reading. Certain evenings Willie Cook would stop by to offer me a drop of Scotch or Kentucky bourbon. He kept the bottles under his desk. 'It's for when Molly and Don start to prickle,' he said. 'After all,' he added, 'the printing press was born from a press used for wine, and only a total drunk like Gutenberg could have invented it.'

For months, for me, the world melted away in the corner of that big room smelling of ink and paper. I found myself perfectly at home there and always marvelled when, at the end of the day, I had to return to the room I'd rented near the port. On the tram home, descending from the other side of the city, I stared out listlessly, incredulous, as if reality was rather more incomprehensible than all the stories I manipulated by fishing out little letters from a wooden case. Reality was the blue mist that enveloped San Francisco daily, and I began to realize it had become something I could no longer bear to pass through.

One day, working on the final pages of a new novel I'd found particularly enthralling, I locked the protagonist, Martin Eden, in the cabin of a ship, preventing him from destroying himself in the event he had a mind to do so. Then I rose from my chair and went to find Willie Cook to submit my resignation.

'I wanted to thank you,' I told him,' because I've truly enjoyed my time here.'

Willie wearily rested his black gloves on the desk.

'I knew you'd leave one day, my boy.'

'I'm sorry, I do like the job…'

'Good luck, Charlie.'

'Thank you, Willie, I'll need it. If I could ask you just one favour, though: there are only a few pages left to go in the book I was working on. Send it to press as is. I've got a bad feeling about the main character and wouldn't want him to do anything foolish.'

'You know that's not possible, Charlie.'

'I'll pay you back for your losses one day. Please, Boss, I promise.'

Willie Cook paused and understood.

'Well, if this is your last request, Charlie, I guess the author will just have to come to terms with it.'

'Feel free to give him my name, when he comes to complain. In fact, I wouldn't mind having a chat with him about it when I'm back.'

'I'll be waiting for you, Charlie.'

'Sooner or later...'

'I'll see you again, I'm sure of it.'

Willie stood up and embraced me, even with the fingers he lacked.

Interior, Night.
24 December 1973

The Tramp tries the barber act.

He dips a brush into a metal bowl full of shaving foam and applies it to a lampshade, distributing the foam evenly over the fabric cylinder. He gazes upon the result with satisfaction, then pretends to wash his hands. He wipes them on his jacket. He takes a razor from the desk and begins rapidly to sharpen it on the strop, spreading his arms out wide, accordion-style.

DEATH (*speaking from the armchair*): It's not funny, Tramp.
                I'm not laughing.

The Tramp concentrates on his work as if he hadn't heard. With precise, deliberate motions, he tries to remove the foam from the lamp. After each pass he runs a white handkerchief over the blade.

CHARLIE: Have you ever had a dog?
DEATH: A dog? Me? As if I could take care of a dog,
              with everything I have to do…
CHARLIE: That's a shame, because it would have done you

good. Dogs have a great sense of humour.

DEATH: What do you mean?

CHARLIE: It would have made you feel less lonely, and improved your personality.

DEATH: Don't be absurd.

CHARLIE: Once I had to pick a dog out at the pound for a film. You know how I can't stand seeing animals locked up. His name was Mut. He loved me so much that when I had to be away for a few days he died of heartache.

DEATH: That's enough nonsense now.

CHARLIE (*annoyed*): This is a barbershop, and in a barbershop anyone can talk all he wants.

DEATH: Go and get ready, Tramp, and get rid of that ridiculous moustache. You've already lived two more years than you had coming to you.

CHARLIE: I'd like to keep the moustache if you don't mind.

DEATH: I wouldn't act so proud if I were you, Hitler wore his the same way.

CHARLIE: Yes, and I made a movie based precisely on this coincidence.

DEATH: Is it also a coincidence that he was born just four days after you? He could almost be your twin brother…

CHARLIE: If he'd become a comic actor, and had the talent for it, it would have been better for everyone. But I don't quite see what you're trying to say…

DEATH: That everything has its double.

CHARLIE: Tyrants and clowns may have the same face, but
           they're not the same person. Luckily, I ended up
           with a mask that only makes people laugh.

DEATH: Your innocence is exasperating.

CHARLIE: I wouldn't want anyone to confuse the two, but
           I freely admit that a lot of people behave badly
           in this world.

DEATH: Time to close up shop, barber.

CHARLIE: Okay, okay. What a hurry you're in.

*The Tramp ignores him, but suddenly notices he's no longer seeing
properly. He starts to sweat. He's obliged to put on his eyeglasses,
but even with them he continues to have problems. At this point
Death rises and places a hand on his shoulder from behind.*

DEATH: Let's go, old chap, it's time…

*The Tramp nods dolefully, wipes off the last of the foam on Death's
cloak, then begins to clean the razor as well, but his hand slips and
lashes out wildly, its trajectory uncontrollable. With this single
motion he neatly severs one of Death's skeletal fingers.*

CHARLIE (*covering his lips*): Sorry.

*The Tramp is mortified. He kneels down and retrieves the phalanges
– proximal, intermediate, and distal – from the floor. He holds
them up and stares, aghast. Death can't believe his eyes either.*

DEATH: Well, that's a slapstick number worthy of your
           pal Stan Laurel.

CHARLIE: I didn't do it on purpose.

DEATH: Never mind. It's not like I've got any blood to spill.

CHARLIE: And now I finally know what it means to feel the hand of Death.

DEATH: ...

From the deep darkness of his hood comes a strangled sob. He tries to stop himself, but finally has no choice but to surrender.

DEATH: Ha. Ha ha. HA HA HA HA HA!

Once again the laughter fades, leaving a stupefied old clown standing in front of a lamp, staring blankly at the tiny pile of bones in his shrivelled palm.

THIRD REEL

And so I arrived in the *Ciudad de la Iglesia de Nuestra Señora de Los Angeles sobra la Porziuncola de Asís*. Now you understand why they shortened the name to just *Los Angeles*. I took a room at the Los Alamitos, a little hotel near the Great Northern. It was run by a man with widely spaced eyes and a large mouth. His motto was 'There's no room for hobos at Mr Hood's.' I gave him a deposit to reassure him. For a short time my feet were free to scamper as they pleased through the city streets, without obligations or set hours. I loved to pick out women from the crowds, to watch them standing in front of a shop window and guess everything about them: age, occupation, tone of voice, the way they would have sat down on a bed or crossed their legs in a restaurant. Sometimes I'd send a smile in their direction, but without any real aim, and I was simply happy if one reciprocated as she moved away in the evening light. I felt wonderfully at ease down there in LA. I was a foreigner among foreigners, and yet somehow for the first time at home. The spring air made me feel euphoric. And it was that same euphoria, along with my own serene solitude, that I recognized in the anonymous multitude surrounding me. It was only when I passed the sign for a theatre that I felt something clutch at my heart, but it was enough for me to quicken my pace and it was forgotten.

Even though I had quit Willie's print shop, I decided that I wouldn't stop furthering my education, which remained very poor. From the moment I ceased to make books I began to buy them from second-hand dealers. I'd always had a weak spot for stalls full of yellowed volumes smelling of basements. Now that I knew all about the work that went into them, it made me suffer to see them abandoned on some makeshift table on the street, it seemed an injustice. I would choose, and allow myself to be chosen by, the ones that cost the least – typically, old philosophical treatises or yoga manuals – and read them furiously, from cover to cover, with no rhyme or reason because I had no teachers. Letters, dialogues, fragments, the diaries of seducers... The names of Epicurus, Plato, Kierkegaard, Nietzsche became as familiar to me as drinking companions.

Much more rapidly than I'd anticipated, however, I spent all the money I'd earned during those months on books. The day my rent came due I found myself with just ten cents in my pocket. I left Mr Hood my suitcase and all my belongings as collateral, but not my violin. 'I don't know what I'd do with your books,' he said. 'But I'll give you a day, otherwise you'll never see your underwear again.'

I went walking down Carson Street with no destination in mind. When I felt tired I stopped and sat down on a bench and analysed the situation. Through the trees, I saw, a line of torches lit up a square. All the restaurant tables were full. The people looked happy. I could only guess what it was like, to sit down in a restaurant without first carefully checking the price of every dish and determining which you could order and which you couldn't. Every woman's voice, every tinkle of glasses provoked in me a sense of unbearable regret for everything I'd never tried. I found myself once again with an empty stomach and I was nearly on the verge of tears when someone, an old negro, sat down next to me. The sun setting behind him lit up his white hair in an arc above his head. One of his ears was half missing.

'Your father happy with you, friend?' he said.

I shivered. What right did this man have to ask me such a question? I don't know why, but I answered him: 'My father is dead.'

The negro remained silent but did not lower his gaze. His breath pearled the air with alcohol and his eyes were the yellowest I had ever seen. I lost patience and turned my back on him. That drunk must have been sent to me by my father himself, from Hell or wherever he ended up. Yet it was hardly likely: my father had never been around when we needed him before, and now my mother was sewing gloves in a lunatic asylum, hitting people and seeing the River Jordan flow across the floor…

The negro continued to study me. I was already on my feet when he stopped me with a hand.

'Wait, friend, I want to give you something. Must be your lucky day. Take this.'

He drew a crumpled piece of paper from his pocket, flattened it with two fingers, then handed it to me. It was a newspaper clipping, hardly legible. A job opening.

The negro's laughter boomed out.

I looked more closely. The Levy Fritz Mutoscope Company, said the scrap of paper, was looking for someone to write title cards. In all the time I'd been poring through newspaper ads, this was the strangest one I'd read.

'I'd hurry over there now, I were your age. Too old for them now, but you're not. Just have to be careful. You see this docked ear of mine? Was a tiger tore off what's missing. Miracle I got outta there alive.'

I was wasting my time. The man was mad. Now he'd started to speak, it seemed he wouldn't stop.

'Happened time I was working as a tamer in the Barnum and Bailey show. You can't trust circuses: sooner or later they'll tear your heart out. I got out just in time. The cinematograph, though, that's the greatest circus ever existed. It'll suck out all our souls.'

'Okay,' I said, 'now how about you go home and get some sleep.'

'People like me ain't got no home.'

I searched my jacket for my last ten cents, without success.

'Sorry, it must have fallen through a hole in my pocket.'

The negro shrugged his shoulders.

I took his hand and closed the coin in his fist.

'I was joking,' I said. 'But it's everything I have.'

'Me too, now.'

We started laughing, like a pair of children.

'One more thing, 'fore you're off. If you get into that world of the cinematograph, don't believe what you hear: there's no way white folks could've invented it. Friend of mine, horseman from Barnum's, knew the man who did, and he warn't no Loomy-air. I could tell you a story…'

'I know, my friend.'

His teeth sparkled.

'Good,' he said. 'Remember that every coincidence has a soul.'

'I won't forget it.'

He squeezed my arm, and his big yellow eyes followed me to the end of the street.

That was my last dime and I'd used it to buy a newspaper ad that sounded like a lottery ticket:

WANTED: Title Card Writer
for the Cinematograph
Levy Fritz Mutoscope Company
Tamarind Avenue

Well, it wasn't as if I had any plans for the evening; I might as well head straight over. Naturally enough, the offices of the Levy Fritz Mutoscope Company were located on the other side of Los Angeles, and already then the city was too vast even for legs as trained up as mine. It took me three hours to get there, and I never would have found it if I hadn't been led through a suburb of identical low houses by a party of Irishmen belting out a ballad about the independence of their island from the United Kingdom. 'If you was English,' one said to me, 'there wouldn't be no leaving here for you tonight.' I made my farewell using the few words of French I knew.

There was nothing the least bit exotic or tropical about Tamarind Avenue. It smelled only of oily sludge and the countryside, of humid darkness. I followed it for a stretch, passing through a mist that left my nose wet. My muscles felt as heavy as concrete, but from time to time bright flashes appeared in the sky, distracting me. After dragging my feet through the mud for some time, I reached a black wrought-iron gate. To one side a brick column bore a sign that read:

> ### LFMC
> ### Cinematographic Production Company

I felt the same joy as when I completed a marathon. Beyond the gate, as far as I could make out, were two giant industrial sheds, and a dark-stained fence surrounding a kind of campanile or control tower, where the offices must be. My first impression was of barracks or an abandoned factory. All the buildings were veiled with fog, which, however, seemed to be lifting. I looked for a reasonably dry place to rest. The only spot to offer any shelter was a corner of the wall at the entrance. I sat down on the ground and leaned back against the wall. I closed my eyes and imagined myself lying on a beach, just like Jimmy the Fearless would have done, with the waves tickling my feet and face. I fell asleep almost immediately.

I was woken by a gentleman in livery. The sun shone full in my face.

'Hey, tramp, get your feet out of the way, we're coming in.'

It took me a while to bring the situation into focus. The gate had been opened and before me stood the longest motorcar I had ever seen in my life: a limousine. I stood up and dusted myself off.

The gentleman in livery returned to his place behind the wheel.

I didn't move.

The man slammed on the horn twice, but my right leg simply drew back a step. I wouldn't have budged an inch even if I were faced with the Seven Trumpets of the Apocalypse or the boss of the whole shebang.

I heard a window being lowered. I planted my feet in the dust and took up a defensive position, as I had done so many times in the ring, ready to receive a blow, spinning my fists. Out of the window appeared a fat-faced man with a white beard. He spoke a single word, but it wasn't addressed to me. With terrible slowness, the long black car began to move. I trembled all over. The bonnet approached dangerously close to my thighs.

'You'll create a real mess on the motorcar, bum,' said the man from the window then.

'If that's a joke, it's not a funny one.'

'You'd like to play the hero, boy, but you're trembling.'

'I am not trembling.'

'You are quite visibly trembling.'

'You're wrong, sir.'

Meanwhile the car continued to push me backwards. Twice I came close to slipping.

'Who are you?'

'I... It's a bit awkward to answer like this.'

I was out of breath.

'Don't kid yourself, I only need to know so that I can alert your mother about the ugly accident you're about to have.'

'My mother's not here, and if you really wanted to get a message to her you would have to cross the ocean,' I panted. 'But even in that case, I'm not sure if she'd bother to listen to you.'

93

'Your name.'

'My name is Charles Spencer Chaplin and I am a title card writer. I heard that they're looking for one around here.'

The car suddenly stopped.

'I read the ad yesterday and hurried over. I wanted to be the first in line – that's why I slept here last night.'

'It's a moving story, but you're behind with the news, Charles. The interviews were scheduled for last week.'

'In that case, sir, go ahead and run me over,' I said quietly.

'That won't be necessary. Last week no one showed up.'

It seemed to me that something had softened in his voice.

'And now step aside. I'll expect you in my office in half an hour. But first clean yourself up: I don't like dusty people, Chas.'

That's what he called me, from then on.

Half an hour later I was sitting in front of his desk, in the middle of a round office. Enormous windows circled the walls, allowing for a 360-degree view over the area, except where some theatrical posters had been hung to block the light. The principal seemed even fatter in his office than he had in the car. His short curly hair and beard created a halo of brighter white around his jowly, milky fair face. He removed his eyeglasses and rubbed a thumb over his eyelids.

'Where do you come from, Chas?' he said.

'I'm from London, but I've been living in America for the past few months.'

He opened his right eye: my appearance clearly betrayed the state of my finances.

'My name is Fritz, Abraham Levy Fritz, and I'm the money behind this operation.'

'I suspected as much, Mr Fritz.'

'How'd you decide to work in the cinema, Chas?'

It was a tricky question, but I recalled what the mime Marceline had said, the first time I'd heard the word.

'It's the invention of the century, Mr Fritz.'

Mr Fritz seemed satisfied.

'My friends are convinced I'm throwing my money out the window,' he said, 'and my mother would like to cut off my access to the family wealth. It's less than a year since I bought this land and we built the studios. Five short pictures so far, zero profit. But it takes time. People who know the business, people with experience… Who have you worked with?'

I held up my hands. I could feel my legs still trembling. My pants were fluttering like a flag.

'I worked in Britain,' I said, 'and then up north, near Chicago. First as a dancer, then an actor, and finally as an assistant director a few times, with Francis Boggs and Thomas Persons.'

By some miracle, those names had remained stuck in my memory after having seen one of their films in a nickelodeon in Albuquerque, the first time I'd ever read words projected against a wall. It had only cost me five cents, and it bought me the notes of an accordion, floating through the air; an hour of smoke, dust, and darkness; the emotion of sitting next to a woman, the noise of the projector, and that sword of light that cut through the room…

'A pianist friend of mine,' I continued, 'became upset with me one evening and threw a glass of whisky at me, said that ever since they introduced all those title cards into the films, it was like having broken all the musicians' thumbs.'

Mr Fritz touched his eyeglasses. I had no idea what kind of job he was offering me, but the story about the pianist was true. We'd played together for a while after he'd been fired from the Royal, El Paso's first movie house, but he'd lost his job because of alcohol, not because of words on a canvas.

I screwed up my courage and went on.

'In order to sum up a scene in a single sentence, you've got to be fast, terse,' I said. 'The audience has to understand at a glance what has happened or is about to happen, where the action takes place, and the relationships between the characters. A lot depends on the director and the actors, of course, but a good part of the film's success depends on these details as well.'

I spoke off the cuff, hoping that the profession was so new that no one yet understood what it consisted of. But it was like trying to ice skate for the first time. And then there was the fact that I didn't actually believe that pantomime needed directions. Pantomime is a dance. Standing there in front of Mr Fritz, I should have been putting myself forward as an actor, but the memory of my New York fiasco still burned the soles of my feet like a rusty clothes iron.

'I fired your predecessor,' said Mr Fritz, 'because he had grammatical errors in his first title. None of us realized, occupied as we were by everything else. People started laughing and kept on laughing. It was supposed to be a serious film – it became a comedy. Tell me, how do you get on with grammar?'

'Very well, Mr Fritz. I corrected proofs in a print shop and literature has always been my passion.'

'Let's not waste any more time, then. We're working on a

film adapted from Dickens. *David Copperfield*. Do you know the story?'

'Inside out.'

'Would you be up to starting with that? It's my idea to begin with the titles this time.'

'The first step's mine?'

'Could be.'

I didn't answer right away. I didn't want to let on how interested I was in the job. Mr Fritz clearly needed something more than simple card writing, he just didn't want to pay very much. His offer arrived promptly.

'Would sixteen dollars a week suit you?'

'I came to California because this is where the cinematograph will put down its roots. But at sixteen dollars a week there won't be any harvest for me.'

'You're an enterprising fellow, Chas.'

'Certainly when it comes to financial matters.'

'How much do you want?'

'Twenty-five and I start right away.'

'I don't know… The others will be angry if I pay you so much. After all, we don't even know who you are.'

'So hire me at sixteen, with a month in advance. But when I finish your *Copperfield* you'll increase my wage to twenty-five.'

Mr Fritz leaned back. I feared the chair would collapse at any moment. His shoes, black and shiny like a businessman's, squeaked.

'Agreed,' he said.

I rose and performed the best bow I could manage.

The Los Angeles central library had wide blue curtains. The semi-circular reading room resembled a theatre. I always sat in the same spot, at the table under the first window, as I tried to devise an approach to the work. I'd requested everything they had on Dickens and *David Copperfield*, and a librarian who liked to hear me talk about London during her lunch hour began to allow me to take one book a night home with me, unbeknownst to her colleagues.

By then I had returned to the Los Alamitos Hotel to retrieve my underwear and settle my account. I no longer cared to see the face of Mr Hood. In Bunker Hill, I found a cheap room and paid for a month. Better to be cautious, better not to tempt fate. At night, the blanket stank slightly of ammonia, but for those first few days I thought it was the most comfortable bed in the world. Now that I had the advance money, I no longer had any problem paying to take buses. I let my dimes wander freely around my pockets, and hearing them jingle as I walked cheered me. I bought myself some new sheets, naturally, and a used jacket with green velvet at the wrists and collar, because mine was too worn and no longer appropriate to my new job. I'd taken it off a second-hand dealer in Hancock Park for a few dollars, with a discount if I listened to some of his poems. It had seemed like a reasonable deal to me. For the past few days, words had had a price for me as well. I suggested he might swap round a few adjectives and change the titles. He was so happy that he lopped another half dollar off the price of the jacket.

In the library, time passed quickly. The problem was the evenings in my room. In only a week I had reread the entire book and learned much of the final chapter by heart. After supper I would recite it to the wife of my hotelier, a tiny woman with shrivelled ears who always bent her head to one side to listen to me, but I still had no idea what was the right thing to do. I bought two small notebooks and decided to try two different paths.

In the first notebook, I began writing about everything, haphazardly: the names of characters, the colour of their hair, dates of birth, the adjectives Dickens used most often, and sentences I'd particularly liked. The second notebook, on the other hand, I left blank, for the final text.

One notebook gradually filled, the other remained empty, and I was unnerved twice over: in the first I was writing too much; in the second I wasn't writing at all. I'd promised myself to sum up nine hundred pages in ten cards. A few letters on a black background. I knew what the first letters would be. *Once upon a time...* that's how all stories started, I couldn't go wrong. But after that? Well, I trusted my instincts.

I decided I had to pick out the objects that appeared in the book and that could be reproduced in Mr Fritz's giant sheds. Books are full of things, but to extract them it's necessary to treat each chapter as if it were a cellar or an attic, with their family relics, implements that have been abandoned and those still in use. I lost two days, but by the end I had drafted a list four pages long. I read it again from the beginning. At the top I'd written these three words:

An overturned boat

It was the home of Mr Peggotty, the Copperfield house-keeper's brother. A barge turned upside down and used as lodging, the only happy place in the entire story. I'd seen it in the library's illustrated edition. Dickens in fact describes the grounded boat as right side up, but I took the liberty of following the artist in this irresistibly poetic detail. I thought that there had to be some connection between that happiness and the fact that the house was upside down. And that people would understand that.

I had my first title:

Once upon a time
there was
an overturned boat…

Three days later I climbed the stairs to Mr Fritz's office. He was standing at the window and gazing out. At the crumbling buildings of the city's outskirts. At the timber yards surrounding his studios. He began to speak without turning around.

'You have to be crazy to believe there's money to made with a white sheet hung on a wall.'

'There are plenty managing to do just that, Mr Fritz.'

'I know, I know… But we're cursed with bad luck, Chas. Yesterday the star of the Dickens picture fell off a ladder and broke his leg. He has accident insurance in his contract. His salary will be paid for another two months, but in the meantime the film won't be made. This was the project I was counting on.'

A small black spider crossed his desk.

'I've brought you what you asked for, Mr Fritz.'

'Leave everything on my desk,' he said.

'It's only two pages. I typed them on a coin-operated type-writer at the Los Angeles library.'

'Two pages? I'm paying you sixteen dollars a week for just two pages?'

'If I'd managed to get it down to one page you would've had to pay me much more, Mr Fritz. Don't you know that it takes more time to write a short letter than a long one?'

'You're one insolent fellow, Chas, as I've told you before.'

'Nature made me short so that I'd never have to kneel down before anyone.'

Mr Fritz began to laugh. It must have been the first sunny moment he'd had that gloomy morning.

'Sorry, Chas, you're right, I'm just feeling out of sorts.'

The old man had apologized to me. He could have fired me for having demanded a raise, and instead he apolo-gized.

'Tomorrow we'll start shooting your film, Chas. I can't bear to hear my mother say again: I told you so, little Abraham, the cinematograph is a toy that will soon break.'

The spider lowered itself from one of the curving desk legs.

'I'll give you two weeks and the raise you asked for.'

'For what, Mr Fritz?'

'To shoot the film, Chas, what the hell else? Didn't you tell me you worked as an assistant director in Chicago? Well, this is your chance. Isn't that what everyone in the country wants? You've got the personality to succeed. All the project needs is a director.'

I cursed my big mouth. I would have had trouble finding Chicago on a map.

'Do you mean to say it should be me…?'

'Don't you know the saying? No matter how you try to hide, destiny will always find you. I bet you've already shot the film in your head, these past few days…

My world was overturned, like the boat in *David Copperfield*.

'But… the actors?'

'I certainly don't pay them to attend to their colleague's recovery. You'll use the troupe that hasn't been able to work, but you'll have to make it happen in two weeks at the most, not a day longer. Get right to work. Go to Henry and ask him for everything you need. He'll give it to you.'

The place was overrun with madmen, I thought, or with desperate ones, if they gave their trust to a stranger discovered sleeping on the ground one morning in front of the madhouse gate.

'I'll go and meet the team,' I said decisively. But my voice as it emerged sounded hoarse and uncertain. Mr Fritz wished me luck.

Leaving the command tower was like stepping into the empty space of an elevator shaft. It was much worse than with the titles. I'd never even seen a movie camera or a strip of celluloid.

My tour with Henry, the chief property man, who wore short-sleeved shirts and braces made of hemp twine, was rather less than encouraging. All I had at my disposal was a pair of sets for the exteriors: two ridiculous house facades and a street corner that wouldn't have fooled a child. But in the back of his shed Henry had recreated a bourgeois drawing room with such accuracy that the only thing missing was the servants. Everything else was there. The credenza with ground glass, the velvet armchairs, a ficus next to the window, the wallpaper, the table with a raised edge and inlaid chessboard. A large part of the work I'd done in my room had just become useless. It wasn't the objects in Dickens's book that I should have transcribed, but the ones filling the giant sheds of the Levy Fritz Mutoscope Company. This was the place to start. There was no choice, and at least my film would have one interior.

But I had not yet taken into consideration the actors.

Henry called them together in the equipment room. I introduced myself with a few blunt words.

'My name is Charles and we'll be spending the next two weeks together. It's not much time.'

The men stared back with ostentatious expressions of scorn. They surely considered me too young for them. A joke from the boss. They would never accept my authority.

'Whoever isn't on board can leave immediately,' I said.

'You're the one who's leaving, tenderfoot.'

The speaker was a tall bloke with black hair, combed straight back.

'My name is Charles, as I said, and I'm no longer inter-ested in what yours is. Who else wants out?'

I had responded quickly enough not to leave him time to react. I had to retain the initiative.

He theatrically feigned a laugh.

'I'm not here to follow the whims of a novice.'

'Certainly, the woes of an old-timer are so much more amusing.'

His eyes flushed with indignant rage, but I too felt my

blood beginning to boil at the situation I'd got myself into. The man came towards me with his arms raised. I put my guard up and assumed a defensive stance. The man quickly sized me up. Though small, I must have looked a fairly robust and solid man, because a few yards from me he turned on his heels and headed for the door, his feet stomping on the wooden floorboards. Later that afternoon, Henry informed me that I had just excluded from the set the second-highest-paid actor in the group, after the one with the broken leg. 'Maybe that'll make Mr Fritz happy,' I exclaimed, shrugging my shoulders.

What Mr Fritz would not be happy about, was the rest of the affair: as the black-haired actor left, he called his faithful followers out by name. In just five minutes I managed to lose a third of the troupe.

I had to resist bursting into tears amidst the pungent odour of varnish, leather, and plaster. I've always made a drama out of everything, and my morale has never ceased to seesaw between euphoria and despondency. I'm usually saved by enthusiasts, their courage, their craziness, but who could be my allies here?

Once again I reviewed my options. Three men of a certain age, grey and frightened; a pair of rather insignificant women; a man with something grotesque about his face and body. Third-rate vaudeville performers. Low-cost rejects from failed companies, not even good as extras. Amazing that they were still around. How was I going to obtain from this group Mr Micawber, the lawyer Wickfield, the clerk Uriah Heep, Dora and Agnes…?

And who would play young master Copperfield?

A woman with carrot-coloured hair approached and bent towards my ear.

'If you give me the lead role, I won't say nasty things behind your back.'

I blushed.

'You'll play Peggotty,' I replied, 'you've got her hair.' But my voice was cracking.

'We'll see each other again tomorrow, at Henry's, nine o'clock,' I said to the others in the thinnest of voices. 'Thank you, anyway, for not abandoning me.'

My tone was a bit pathetic, but something like a hint of curiosity flashed in their eyes.

'Can you still manage it, with the group reduced like this?' Henry asked once we were alone.

'I'll find a way to enlarge it, it's just the lead that's missing,' I lied.

'Bit late to be engaging him.'

'For now, just take me to the workshop. The other day I saw some carpenters on the job.'

The next morning I arrived on my first set with the shaky step of a man who has tossed and turned a hundred times between the sheets without managing to get a moment's sleep, but is nonetheless sure that somewhere or other he has some clear ideas. The actors remaining after the previous day's exodus, along with Henry and Ricardo, a technician of Argentinean origin and a greater stutterer than Grogan, awaited me with suspicious punctuality. They wished, with ill-concealed relish, to observe a man's destruction. Perversely, the spectacle seemed to put them in a good mood.

I placed myself at the centre of the group and one by one looked them in the eye.

'If I fail, people,' I said in the surliest manner I could manage, 'we're all out of here. Mr Fritz has told me there won't be any more chances. So, welcome, to your last film.'

I hoped I'd managed to frighten them, or at least provoke them into some small show of pride. I was mistaken. Henry was the best property man in California and wouldn't have had trouble finding another job; the others would have been just as happy getting soused in a Mexican tavern.

'Let's get shooting,' I said with enthusiasm I didn't feel. The motley crew followed me with some reluctance.

I know it sounds unlikely, but in just two weeks I learned everything I needed to know about light sources, about how interminable a celluloid reel can be, about the way to call a scene and then cut it, and how to look through the hole of a motion picture camera, which, if you turn even slightly, makes the people come out distorted... But what I knew already was that no title card could ever convey more than an actor could with the smallest gesture, simply an eyebrow raised at the right moment, or the bare hint of a trembling lip. I also knew how to work within a group, how it was possible to survive in the chaos of a travelling circus by pretending to be part of a real troupe. And beyond everything else that I brought to that film, I knew London, the London of the southern neighbourhoods, of the slums, of the orphanages and the theatres, of the cold garrets between Lambeth Road and Southwark, of the queues in front of the agencies, of the pickle factories and slaughterhouses. I had seen with my own eyes what Dickens was talking about when he described humiliation and exploitation. If I got out of bed on the right side, I convinced myself that it was as if they'd called on one of Dickens's own characters to direct the film. But this rarely happened – I simply had too much to deal with.

Henry and I toiled with the other workers day and night to prepare a credible set. I made them tear down and rebuild a dozen times until I was satisfied. Thinking back now, it was nothing more than a T-junction and an ill-proportioned, poorly lit square, evoked with just a few wooden beams hammered together, three street lamps, a crumbling sandstone wall, a pair of gutters that were falling apart, and some old doors. But for me it was a whole neighbourhood that came back to life: the arches of Canterbury Music Hall, the police station, the portal of the Church of Christ where my mother prayed, its big window illuminated even at night for the funeral ceremonies, the doctor's office, the small windows of a pub, a porcelain shop, the electric sign for Ziegfeld Roof, the corner of Baxter Hall, where for a penny I'd had a slice of lemon cake and attended a magic lantern show… In short, the entire topography of my memory.

On instinct, I entrusted the role of David Copperfield to the youngest worker on site. He came from Wales and had worked in a coal mine. At least he won't sweat under pressure, I thought; Charles Dickens would be pleased.

At night, in my room, I wrote the screenplay, on production company letterhead. After a few days, the set was so crowded with extras of English origin, recruited from among the other workers, that I got in the habit of exaggerating my cockney accent. I also called in a little group of deaf-mute actors to join the production, letting everyone see just how well I understood them. Life itself had taken care to teach them the art of pantomime. It was an unintentional move that ultimately bore fruit. The actors that had been with us from the beginning began to get nervous and, after having disdainfully refused to cooperate, finally rolled up their sleeves and started giving their all. With people it's never merely a question of money.

I filled scenes with beggars, fraudulent blind men, red-nosed clowns like the ones who worked in second-tier music halls, stray dogs, negro prostitutes with big black breasts strolling along the banks of an invisible Thames, fruit vendors struggling to pull their carts of apples and tomatoes along a stretch of street I'd had spread with tar and wet down… I put a Bible into someone's hand. I used rouge to thicken the women's lips and I blackened the little boys' teeth. I placed a little old man in front of a coffee cart with a Barbary barrel organ and sat a band of idlers down on a step. I even recreated the shop window of the Sharps photography studio on Westminster Bridge Road and decorated it with set photos. (Some years earlier, the shop had displayed a photo from when I was with Casey's Court Circus, and this had filled me with wonder and given me a taste of the pomegranate flavour celebrity would have for me.)

I gave everyone clear, concise instructions. But each day was like stepping up onto the high beams of a skyscraper under construction, with no railings. In the first take an actor playing a beggar thanked an extra for her charity with an excessive nod of the head. I leapt onto the set like a Saracen. 'There's no place here for courtesies,' I yelled. 'These people no longer feel anger or gratitude – so no gimmicks. We need restraint here, we need the truth. Think about the scene, and remember the eyes of thousands of spectators are trained on you. Hams can make their way to the exit, I've always despised them.'

I was laying it on pretty thick, and yet what I wanted from even the most minor player was maximum economy in their movements. I was asking them to be natural, not to pose, not to go over the top. Nearly seventy years on, I still get annoyed by the way people confuse acting and exhibitionism. I've spent a lifetime trying to demonstrate that an actor is something else, something small and silent but full of expression, without straining or attention-seeking or deception.

That morning on set, the crew looked at me as they might have looked at a rhesus monkey in the zoo. But I was quite serious about it. I had promised myself that I would use this film to exorcise my demons, and now I was bringing them all back, professional and personal. I would draw them out by the hair from the leaky top hat of my memories or from wherever else they had ended up, even if some of them, by then, had already been laid to rest. I was down there in California, between the orange groves and the desert, to show the world how awful life can be for some human beings.

In a month the picture was done.

I called it *The Ballad of the Upside Down House*, and for the first time in my life I was proud of something. I invited the whole troupe for tea to celebrate, but no one showed. Overcome with weariness, I fell asleep with my arms on the table, among the steaming teapot, empty cups, and uneaten crumpets.

But the worst was still to come. When we projected the

film for Mr Abraham Levy Fritz, his reaction was so violent that I would have preferred to find myself in the ring with the Galveston Giant than with this appalling subspecies of drunken bear. Mr Fritz began to berate first Henry, and then, one by one, all his staff. With the punctiliousness of an accountant, he finished up by amply insulting President Taft and all the stars of the American flag, too. Now that he was properly warmed up, he turned towards me. I grabbed my jacket and headed for the exit.

'Charles Spencer Chaplin,' I heard him say behind me, 'have you at least ensured that the title cards are free of grammatical errors?'

I came to a halt halfway between his desk and the door, and gave him one last look.

'The premiere is set for the Empire Theatre next week, and it's too late now to cancel,' he said, suddenly throwing a startling series of punches at his own head.

I took a step back.

'You'll be there,' he growled, 'and if the audience and the critics decide to rip you to pieces on the spot, I'll be there to lend a hand,' he concluded, unleashing a fearful right at his crown.

He was not the first person I had ever seen cover his head with punches, nor did it make much of an impression on me this time. My gypsy grandmother's sister used to bash herself whenever something went wrong, and so did a lot of boxers, to keep themselves awake during a bout. But I could tell that the real target of Mr Fritz's anger was still me – the execution had not been avoided, only postponed. All the same I breathed deeply with relief.

'I'll be there, Boss, on time.'

Out of caution, I avoided asking for my twenty-five dollars that week and made sure not to be seen around for a few days. I feared my luck was about to run out once and for all. I packed my bags in my room in Bunker Hill and told my landlady that I would soon be leaving. I figured I could always return to England, or to Willie Cook's. And put behind me for ever this fixation with becoming the greatest actor in the world. I had already seen so much. And yet.

A feeling weighed heavily in my stomach, like an indigestible mouthful – the shame of knowing what would happen at the premiere.

For a week I walked past the Empire Theatre every day, even several times a day, but as if I were just out for a stroll. I was studying the battlefield, all the time knowing that there wouldn't be any battle, just a humiliating defeat.

On the day of the premiere it started to rain at lunchtime. Mr Fritz had done his job well: you could see posters in every neighbourhood in the city, and the newspapers had given the story plenty of inches. There was nowhere in all of Los Angeles where I could have hidden.

From my second-hand dealer friend in Hancock Park I bought a pair of striped trousers, along with a variety of white shirts that had been sold off by a theatre company that had flopped. I was obliged to listen to an entire poem about the voyage of one of his Portuguese ancestors in the South Atlantic, but the discount was considerable.

Thus turned out – with my green jacket and a low-collared, frilly white shirt – I did not pass unobserved. The usher, with a malicious air, stopped me at the entrance to the theatre.

'I'm the picture's director,' I said.

'And I'm Saint Peter,' he said, 'letting people in without a ticket.'

Mr Fritz himself had to intervene to compel the man, now surrounded by an inquisitive crowd, to let me in.

'Welcome to Hell,' said dear Abraham to cheer me up.

Henry and Ricardo escorted me to a box.

'Forgive us, but we have orders to lock you in.'

'It would have been better for me not to come.'

'We've been tailing you for the past three days.'

I heard the sound of the key turning in the lock. Mr Fritz had truly thought of everything.

In the orchestra pit a coloured musician at a cottage upright began to play a melancholy ragtime, and the lights went down. Mozart's *Requiem* would have been cheerier than that insufferable dirge.

In the dark appeared the first titles:

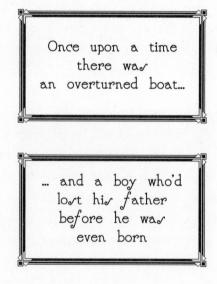

Dream of his
father's death

Peggotty's hair
is the colour
of red coral

His mother forced
to remarry:
the ignorant
condemn her,
the wise are
full of pity...

Mr Murdstone is a
FIRM stepfather

And Mr Murdstone's
sister is a FIRM aunt

At boarding school,
a leather sack on
his shoulders

Discovery of
friendship
and rebellion

My breath:
a mother expires

Orphan

114

Forced labour: wine
warehouses
and the factories
of London

Generosity lives on
at the Micawbers'

The leech cure

The fraudulent clerk
Uriah Heep
wins Mr Micawber's
soul at dice

Flight from London
in a donkey-cart

From Aunt Betsey's
one can see the sea

It takes money
to study

The lawyer
Wickfield's house

Agnes's eyes

Probation

Seduction and
shipwrecks

A child-wife: Dora

The death of Dora
and of her dog,
Jip

Uriah Heep lays
snares for Agnes
and her father

The struggle

> Agnes, why did I
> neglect you?

> Heep's nose
> following his defeat

> The dance of
> Mr Micawber, cleared
> of all debts,
> about to leave for
> another continent

> David's final return
> to England

Curiously, no one since has ever spoken of the film, or otherwise paid any attention to it, and I've been careful myself not to own up to my distant and fortuitous directorial debut. I don't believe a single reel has survived. But the next day there appeared, in the *Los Angeles Times*, an article signed by one Dean Coquetry. I've kept it all these years, and now I'm leaving it here for you. It's a bit crumpled but still legible.

The Ballad of the Upside Down House is an exceptional motion picture. It tells the real story of David Copperfield and not the sugared version we all know. Every scene is at the same time intensely visionary and painfully realistic. Dickens's characters come alive with unexpected power, and the film, frame by frame, gains in dignity and beauty. All eyes in the Empire Theatre remained riveted to the screen until the final scene, amused and moved by turns. When it was over a long silence followed as the stunned spectators found themselves back in a theatre, then the hall exploded into spontaneous and interminable applause. We are confident that certain episodes will endure in the memory of this new art form, which only now begins to discover its extraordinary expressive possibilities. The long sequence recounting the death of Copperfield's father before his own birth is an innovative intrusion of the director's fantasy into the novel's plot. As is the scene in which the moneylender Uriah Heep challenges all the men of his neighbourhood to a game of dice, and diabolically wins their souls. Or the one in which a woman with long raven hair administers a leech cure to the young David during an attack of fever, or the journey in a gig across the gloomy English countryside towards Dover… The film fulfils the best of expectations and will surely be met with favour by both audiences and critics. We may already affirm that the young director of this melancholy but tremendously funny *Ballad* stands out as one of the great new talents of American cinema, on a par with David Wark Griffith. The producer tells me his name is Chas Chaplin. Remember it. You can certainly bet on him in the future.

That evening, a few minutes before the film ended, I'd tried to turn the handle of the door to my box. Mr Fritz must have given the order to unlock it when he realized that, mysteriously, the audience was enjoying the screening, because the door opened wide without resistance. On this occasion, at least, the public would go home happy. Outside the theatre it was still raining. I tore off a strip of the soaking-wet poster that remained standing, barely, on the easel out front. I put it in my pocket, just as I'd done a month earlier with the scrap of paper given to me by the yellow-eyed negro. Who knows why, but at that moment, my mother came to mind, and the steamship that had brought me to America, and I wondered how many oceans I would have to cross before I found my true place in the world.

Mr Fritz had people looking for me all over the city for three whole days. In vain. I returned to his offices myself at the end of the week, but only to draw my salary and be on my way.

'I've been off feeding the geese,' I said to Henry before he could ask me where I'd been hiding, and he doubled over with laughter. Maybe he was simply happy to see me again. Or maybe he was crazy too, like everyone else in that place.

'Go see the boss, he wants to talk to you,' he said, once he had collected himself.

'Okay, best of luck with work, Henry, and say hello to the others for me when you see them.'

'I have a feeling you'll be seeing them yourself very soon.'

'I'm not holding my breath.'

Henry bowed his head and spread his arms. Who knows, maybe he had started to truly care for me.

I had no desire to climb up to the tower office, but since this was the last time I would have to do it, I made an effort. Mr Fritz was as usual seated in his armchair and gazing out.

'I saw you arrive, Chas. I've been expecting you.'

'I only came to be polite,' I told him.

'And for your twenty-five dollars.'

'I earned it.'

'Of course you earned it. And you'll earn much more from now on.'

'No, Mr Fritz, we won't be seeing any more of each other. I'll be on my way.'

'I don't understand.'

'It's a question of logic: if you sit down at a poker table and for once you have the audacious luck to win big, it's better to change tables afterward. It's my rule.'

'You're a wise man, Chas.'

'The few times I've happened to win anywhere I've been in America, I've always left straight away. I'm sorry. I don't see why I shouldn't do so this time.'

'But—'

'It's my fate to leave and to lose things, Mr Fritz. Here

with you, I've found myself under a lucky star, but I don't believe there's anywhere on earth I can tie it down, and there's the problem. The wind has blown favourably, it's been a great adventure, believe me, but it won't last. Why ruin everything pretending to be something I'm not?'

'That's old news, Chas. I knew all about it.'

The fat man was laughing. I had just delivered the most sincere and emotional speech I'd ever made to another human being, and he was laughing. And crying. He pressed his hands to his sagging belly to stop it trembling too much.

'What did you know, Mr Fritz?'

'That you weren't a director, I knew *that* for sure…'

I had to wait a little before Mr Fritz calmed down and was able to continue.

'What did you think? That I don't make inquiries about the people I work with? I knew that you never worked up north, near Chicago. That you'd never been an assistant director, not for Francis Boggs and not for Thomas Persons – they told me so themselves, in person, they're friends of mine. I also knew you'd never written a screenplay or titles in your life…'

'Then why, Mr Fritz?'

'Why? Hell, I don't know, it was a gamble. Call it my nose for business. You were the only one with the guts to go all the way and come back with my dreams intact. You've got loads of ideas in your head, and the thing I appreciate most in a man is inventiveness. But I also knew that you'd got up onstage when you were five, and that you'd worked in a circus… Anyway, this is your new contract: twelve pictures through to the end of next year. Your imagination is the limit – the rest is taken care of.'

'None of this is what you thought the first time you saw the film.'

'Pah. I was scared.'

'I still don't know this profession, Mr Fritz.'

'Now you're the one who's scared.'

'What's the salary?'

'I'll give you a raise of ten dollars a week.'

'Twenty.'

'You're dreaming.'

'It's what I do best. Farewell, Mr Fritz.'

'Twelve, not one dollar more.'

'Eighteen, not one dollar less.'

We settled on fourteen. In the space of a month my balance had gone from ten cents to the dizzying figure of thirty-nine dollars a week.

Outside Henry and Ricardo were waiting for me.

A smile bloomed on each man's mouth like an orchid.

A few days later we were shooting my first western, on 35 mm film, in the Mojave Desert at the edge of the Sierra Nevada. It was the story of an Indian child who gets lost and is adopted by a group of white settlers. When she's twenty some members of her tribe happen to recognize her thanks to a tattoo on her leg. The chief, who had sworn to avenge her disappearance, then decides to attack the white men, kill them all, and burn down their settlement.

Bafflingly, the film filled every nickelodeon in California and a copy was even sold in Pennsylvania, Mr Fritz told me with pride, to the Warner brothers at the Cascade Theatre in New Castle. Things were shaping up well.

I had even found a reliable method of working. Mr Fritz had made available to me a small room in the rear of a warehouse, with a Smith typewriter and a tiny table. Without space it's easier to work, he would say. I would sit down in front of the machine and wait. If necessary I too would give myself a few punches in the head. I only had the piece of paper there in the typewriter as inspiration because I didn't know how to type, not really. But I wouldn't get up until I had a good idea, then I would present it to the others, and we would get right down to it, without second thoughts, without delays, and above all without a script.

Sometimes it was enough for me to kneel down, shut my eyes, and plug my ears, in the middle of the set, in order to visualize, exactly as it would turn out, the scene that we needed to create.

The short films that I shot in this period were about drunk typographers who pour bottles of alcohol into the rotary presses, about thieves redeemed thanks to love, about people who lose their job and fall ill but are saved by a talisman or a book, about children who are mistreated or have paralysed arms and then stumble across a stash of gold, about little seamstresses, journeymen musicians, failed inventors... all somewhat rickety and illogical plots that I've preserved in my head to this day like an archive.

Those films would last a quarter hour each, give or take. We finished as many as three a week, but none of them would appear under my name. If some journalist came asking I would offer an alias as a precaution and produce a factory smile. Some years later, I introduced the custom of including the director's name in a square at the beginning of each film, but only to defend myself against all the Tramp lookalikes in circulation by then.

Actually, I've always thought that anonymity would have been both more fair and more elegant than claiming a credit, because I didn't invent anything. Having little idea where to start, I copied from others. Ricardo and Henry were my guardian angels. Together we studied all the short films coming out – with ever-increasing frequency. There was a great deal of demand: no one could work fast enough to meet it. The only difference was that I copied better than the others. Or more quickly. With greater care. Every film held the kernel of an idea that could be developed, but you needed to see it. Some people couldn't see anything there, because everything was new and the possibilities seemed infinite. No one had yet formalized techniques like the close-up, the detail, the medium-long shot that French critics would later call the *plan américain*, the long shot, the fade, the tracking shot, cross-cutting. But we were already using them. I've always been the instinctive type: intuit something first, study it later.

Sure, I may have had a few minor original ideas myself, but strictly speaking they were always imitations as well – imitations of nature. One afternoon as I edited a sequence in which a man misses a train at Los Angeles station and arrives late to a meeting with the woman of his life, Ricardo was trying unsuccessfully to tell me something, remaining stuck for two minutes on the same word, to the point where he choked and gasped with rage. That was how I invented the stutter edit, or stop-action cinematography. You'd repeatedly roll back the teeth on the machine to produce a curious game of suspense and reduplication. Onscreen the actors moved in fits and starts and I found the results irresistibly funny. But the technique didn't catch on and its discovery was never attributed to either me or Ricardo, the only technician I knew capable of choking himself on a word. In any case, I've never liked special effects. A little man stirring a spoon in a cup of tea is for me more interesting than a great fire. In the same way, I've always preferred shooting the shadow of a train across an actor's face to shooting an entire station.

This was also the period when I began to meet the first stars of Hollywood. I remember the ambiguous round face of Mary Pickford and Blanche Sweet's melancholy one, the perfect nose of Lillian Gish and the delightful impertinence of her sister, Dorothy. In each of them I looked for the adolescent features of Hetty Kelly or the cheerfulness of Alice Sycomore. I even went to dinner with some of them, to Levy's Café or to Barney's place, and sometimes to see a boxing match. They called me *Sharlie*, or *Boodie*, or else *Hon*, but the seducer's trade required more time than I ever had available. I lived in a modest hotel, saved as much as I could, and every so often ate my dinner on the beach. It had only been a few months since *The Ballad of the Upside Down House* and already everyone treated me like someone who had been there from the very beginning.

Interior, Night.
24 December 1974

We see the Tramp from behind. He looks carefully at one of the
pictures on the wall of his room, a portrait of a woman done in
pencil, hanging next to the door. A gift from Picasso. He plays the
part of an old man visiting the Museum. He arches his back, and
with the tips of his fingers, from within his sleeves, he lifts the
black overcoat he's wearing. He balances his hat on the collar.
Slowly he grows taller.

DEATH: If you think you can impress me...
CHARLIE: Once I made a whole class of schoolchildren
           laugh with this trick.
DEATH: Well, I've been out of the nursery for
           centuries...

The Tramp takes off his coat and lets it fall to the ground. He
pulls an apple out of his pocket, bites into it, but realizes that it
has a worm in it. Death is unmoved. The Tramp tosses the apple
away and spins in place, pretending to be trapped in a revolving
door. He comes out dazed. Then he pulls on some boxing gloves. He

bends down to step through the ropes of the ring. He carries a pail into a corner and sits down on a stool. He massages his stomach. When he stands he makes as if to shake hands with everyone: his invisible opponent, the referee, the trainers. He approaches the cloaked figure as well.

DEATH (*icily*): We'll shake hands soon enough.

CHARLIE: You aren't going to wish me good luck?

DEATH: For what?

CHARLIE: For entering a boxing match at my age.

DEATH: You won't last the first round.

CHARLIE: You see how I was right?

DEATH: About what?

CHARLIE: The silent era was better.

DEATH: You're not making me laugh.

The Tramp shrugs his shoulders, mimes the gesture of pulling down the rope to climb into the ring, but his back obliges him to be very careful. He looks around, pretends to flee, but it's as if someone is pushing him from behind.

DEATH: Stop playing the clown, this is serious.

The Tramp suddenly shakes his head, as if someone had rung the bell for the first round. If there were a referee, he would hide behind him, and it would be irresistible, as it always had been, but there's no one else in the room, just him and Death. He tries nonetheless to begin his dance, but his legs are slow. He punches the empty air and bends over, exhausted, but all things considered he acquits himself fairly well.

128

DEATH (*pitiless*): You haven't moved, you know.

CHARLIE (*panting*): I can't take any more. Even when I was young you would have been lucky to see such a scene.

DEATH: You haven't moved. You just imagined it.

The Tramp is crushed. The weight of the gloves causes him to totter. His balance is precarious.

DEATH: Just look at yourself in the mirror.

The Tramp approaches the wall. He's half naked, wearing nothing but a pair of white long johns, his bowler hat, and some worn-out slippers.

DEATH: Now do you believe me?

The Tramp is confused. Wispy white hair covers his chest.

DEATH: Once you made invisible fleas jump inside a box; now you're the dancing flea.

His bare belly sways heavily.

CHARLIE: You see how you are? You always want to have the last word.

DEATH: That's because you can barely remember your lines. Come on, let's put your memory to the test. Could you tell me the names of the Seven Dwarfs?

The Tramp begins to count on his fingers under his breath: Doc, Grumpy, Sleepy… but each time, halfway through, he breaks off and is forced to start over from the beginning. Finally, defeated, he lowers his arms.

Death, in his armchair, puts a hand over his mouth. He lifts it to count on his bony fingers, then covers his mouth again. He appears to be imitating the Tramp.

DEATH: It would have helped if you'd had the strength
            to take your gloves off.

A hysterical titter emerges from inside his cowl. It's like a crack in a wall. A few seconds later it's a hiccup, then a guffaw. Death can no longer control himself.

DEATH: I'll see you next Christmas… (*continuing to laugh
            as he moves away*)

The Tramp is left alone in the centre of the room.

FOURTH REEL

My awakening, as some awakenings are, was abrupt and unforeseeable and happened one still-warm morning in September. Mr Fritz gathered us all together in his little tower office. The letter he had received was open on his desk. He wiped the sweat from his face with an embroidered handkerchief and looked out the window.

'We're being sued by the MPPC.'

'For what?' Henry asked.

'For the same reason they've sued a great many other independent producers – for having used movie cameras that violate the patent laws. We can't distribute any product anywhere in this yellow-bellied land, not even to the tiniest storeroom in Los Angeles. Either we pay them a fee or it's nothing doing.'

'Excuse me, folks,' I interrupted, trying to restore some measure of calm, 'help me to understand, what is this MPPC?'

An alien could not have asked a dumber question. Mr Fritz was the only one to reply.

'It's the Motion Picture Patents Company, Chas, the most powerful trust in the industry. They've got Edison and

American Mutoscope and Biograph, plus a fair number of minor companies like Vitagraph and Lubin. The fact is that they're sharks who want to control everything: distribution, production, the equipment. We even have to use the film stock they say we do, from Eastman Kodak. They couldn't manage to monopolize the market on their own – they tried, the courts have already stopped Edison doing it several times – so they got together, and now they're back on the attack, to clear the field of every last runt who dares challenge them.'

'But what are they accusing us of?'

'Of having used the Latham loop.'

'Whose loop?'

'It's a mechanism in movie cameras.'

'And we used it?'

'Of course, Chas, the cameras you shoot on are the best out there.'

'So they're right?'

'No, you thick-headed Englishman, they're not right. The technology was already part of other cameras' patents. This time, though, they've got enough power to buy up all the courts of appeal in the United States.'

'What if we pay the fee?'

'That's not even funny, Chas. If we submit to their tyranny we're through. There's more than a patent at stake here – they want to close us down. And I'm not strong enough to resist them by myself.'

Mr Fritz mopped his forehead. The sun beat down relentlessly, setting the windows ablaze.

'If I've heard right, there's also one Thomas Alva Edison behind all this,' I said amid the general despondency.

Mr Fritz bowed his head wearily.

I was suddenly thirsty. I picked up a glass of water from the table, took a deep draught, and raised my voice loud enough for everyone to hear.

'The only thing Edison is capable of inventing,' I said to them, 'is the electric chair.'

I was fishing, but I *had* read something about it in a second-hand physics textbook. And the mug on that man... whenever I saw his face in the papers, it had always struck me as belonging to someone with a talent for making money and money alone.

'Men like him do nothing but defraud the world and spout lies.'

The others looked on, suddenly curious. 'The cinema wasn't invented by the Lumière brothers, nor by Edison, and not even by the Germans,' I declared solemnly.

'By who then?'

'By a black man who worked in a circus.'

The group burst into their first laugh of the morning.

'You should be doing my job,' said Brandon, one of the most predictable gag writers in the history of cinema, 'you're pretty good.'

The only one not laughing was Mr Fritz. He always seemed to take me seriously, ever since I pulled off the Copperfield film. He appeared to have limitless faith in my methods.

'Okay, Chas, you're on. Find me this negro wizard of yours as soon as possible, or don't bother to show your face around here any more.'

*

135

For the next week I did nothing but walk the Los Angeles streets. His faith notwithstanding, Mr Fritz had cut my weekly wages back down to sixteen dollars. Plus expenses, he said. With an assignment like yours, you can't complain. On the last day I was so caught up in my thoughts that I only narrowly avoided being run down by a truck loaded with wine barrels.

'Do you always walk in the gutter?' the driver shouted at me.

I did. I'd walked that way since I was a child. At the edge of the road, following the line of the kerb. I had experimented with other variations, skipping about like a boxer, or moving from side to side with the elegant sashay of a torero. But I always ended up walking in my own way, one foot in front of the other. It came naturally to me. Like an acrobat on a wire, always about to fall, I reflected angrily.

I quickened my pace. Before long I was running, out of habit. At the end of the street a group of dustmen were cleaning up the area.

'Hey you, take it easy,' one of them said.

I leaned against a wooden fence.

'I'm out of shape,' I said, panting.

'Where are you running to?'

'I'm going back to England.'

'You'll really have to get back in shape then.'

They laughed a bit, sadly, then returned to their work.

'Actually, we thought you had a free ticket, too,' said the one who had spoken up first.

'A free ticket for what?'

'For tonight's show. You're not the first to come complaining. By the time I started my shift they'd already cleared out. Maybe that's what they always do. They give out free tickets for the last show and then disappear the night before. Take a look. They must be pretty well organized.'

I took the colourful ticket in my hand.

> **Goldstein & Gabor Circus**
> **Free Admission for One Child**
> **Exotic Animals and Freak Show**
> **8:00 PM Lincoln Park**
> **Show Starts on Time!**

'All I know is that I promised my son I'd take him, because a man skinnier than my broom here gave me a pair of tickets. And now they're scrap paper.'

'Did you see them leave?'

The street sweep stopped and raised his head.

'Were you one of them?'

'No, but I realized I might have something to ask them. No one knows where they were headed?'

'They might have gone in any direction. They took off at night, like thieves. No matter how far you run, I'm afraid, you won't be able to catch them.'

'But we're talking about an entire convoy, it couldn't have vanished into thin air.'

'It already has done.'

I gave a look around. The man was right. Only the merest traces of the Goldstein & Gabor Circus remained. A big circle on the ground. Snack wrappers, twine and rope, rags and a few piles of feed. The tracks of animals on the dusty ground. A dead bird. Some abandoned equipment. A single wooden skittle. The scene filled me with an inexplicable anguish beyond all reason. It felt as if everything were about to disappear, even the leaves on the trees. And the goldfish in the ponds. As if all the seesaws in all the parks in Los Angeles were stolen away. As if the universe had suddenly been depopulated.

I was just about to return discouraged to my room when a cloud of dust rose up at the end of the street. It took me a while to bring it into focus. Slowly, one by one, appeared a long line of caravans, two giraffes, an elephant, two men in livery playing tambourines. A fanfare sounded. The multi-colour spectacle of the Gabor Circus. They stopped in front of us, under the stunned gaze of the dustmen. A man in a red wig leapt down from the first car.

'We made a mistake,' he said. 'We had the calendar from last year.'

And he opened his arms.

An unstoppable wave of joy swept over me, from my toes to the crown of my head. It was absurd and unreasonable, but I felt happy. I spent the whole afternoon helping to re-raise the big top. Before they were done I asked who the ringmaster was. They told me it was Mr Gabor and I had them point out where I could find him.

Yitzhak Gabor was sitting on a tiger stool and smoking a Hoyo de Monterrey cigar.

I walked up and said I needed to talk with him.

'Follow me,' he said.

The big top billowed slightly in the wind, like a swollen hot-air balloon. We sat down at the edge of the empty ring and, before I'd had a chance to ask a single question, Mr Gabor began to tell me his story. He'd been born on the road, like all his brothers: he in the village of Pécs, in Hungary; others on the Danube or the Tisza; Janusz, the oldest, on Lake Balaton. His mother convinced herself that the place in which each child had come into the world had determined his character, and she mentally divided them up into river children, lake children, and land children. To each of these categories she had assigned a particular quality that she saw reflected in their nature. She had impetuous children, who spoke in long, meandering curves that often ended up overflowing their banks, and others, like Janusz, who knew how to stay silent for hours, who had the gift of patience and inspired calm and confidence in everyone. 'For me,' said Mr Gabor, 'my mother had foreseen the future of a sedentary man, rooted like an onion in the middle of the orchard. She thought that sooner or later I would have left this life of ours, spent between fairgrounds and animals, and that I would have retired to the country, got married, and built myself a wooden house, because I was a tree child, with my feet stuck in the earth. She couldn't imagine that I'd have come this far, all the way to the New World, or that I'd have seen more water than ever filled the eyes of my brothers, from the day of their birth to the very end. But the way I see it, ultimately she wasn't wrong. It's just that the clay my feet are stuck in isn't the Hungarian countryside but the dusty red earth of circuses the world over...'

I listened to him in silence.

'And what kind of man are you, a tree man or a fish man?'

'I don't yet know, sir, but I too have crossed my ocean.'

'And did you make it to the other side?'

'I don't think so, no, not yet.'

'You know, my mother was a Russian Jew and she met my father in Minsk on tour. He was scheduled to go on after her and he was waiting in the wings – all dressed in white and with a pointed hat – when he saw her. As the audience applauded the end of her performance, my father burst into the ring and stood before her. He declared himself to her in a mixture of all the dialects of Eastern Europe, right there in front of two thousand people. The spectators thought that it was part of the performance and began to laugh. It was an irresistible set-up and after that my parents made it part of their act for years: a white-faced clown professes his love for a contortionist with long hair and a red mouth, and follows her all over the circus, in and out of the spotlight shining on them, all the way to the exit. They played love for laughs. And perhaps this is why I've never taken love too seriously. But one evening my father went to bed complaining of a little stomach pain. He undid his belt and lay down, and the next morning nothing could wake him up. Clowns from all over the Empire came to his funeral, all bundled up with scarves, but still in costume. Some with golden trombones, an enormous curving nose, false eyelashes, others on bicycles and wearing trousers up to their armpits. A little wind-up piano played Italian music. The neighbourhood women called the children to the windows to watch. There'd never been a show like this before. At one point my mother had such a violent laughing attack that she collapsed in convulsions. She became feverish, and just twenty-four hours later she joined my father in his last and definitive act. This is why I've never taken death too seriously either.'

Mr Gabor's laughter beat against the walls of the giant tent and smoke came out of his nose. I wasn't sure why he was telling me all these stories, but his voice was kind and I didn't want to interrupt him.

'My father had taught me how to make people laugh,' he continued, 'and how to make them cry, as well as every other trick a clown or mime might need. He taught me to play the accordion, on a lovely instrument covered with white mother-of-pearl buttons. It closed up like a suitcase and had a black bellows in the middle and a wooden body decorated with curls and arabesques. I've had three accordions in my life. The first I played in front of Emperor Franz Joseph; the second went up in flames, along with the rest of the village, after an attempt to assassinate the Tsar; the third, I didn't bring with me to America: I couldn't risk another fire... But my true talent didn't show itself in either music or mime. It's animals I understand. Even camels obey me without protest. For half a century, I've kept up a continual correspondence with the tiger trainers and elephant trainers of at least two continents; they ask me the wildest things. To judge from the amount of mail I still receive, it appears that I'm the only one capable of knowing an animal's true character merely through a letter. Many tamers have thanked me for having saved their lives. Occasionially, though, my answers arrive too late and I hear from another impresario that their artist has suffered a tragic accident...'

I thought about the yellow-eyed negro with the half-missing ear whom I'd met some months earlier. Could Mr

Gabor have guessed that tiger's true character? But he was carrying right on with his life story. I feared that he would go on talking for ever, but I had time.

'When I first came to America,' Gabor said, 'I worked for a while as a horse expert on William Frederick Cody's Wild West show. The world knew him as Buffalo Bill, but for me he was just an old actor with pale skin and long hair, and a little dagger of a beard on his chin – my friend Billy. Even the Indians who took part in the performance respected my ability to get any colt to take the bit. Sitting Bull himself asked me what my secret was. "I know the language," I told him. Ah, what a show that was, boy: women in the saddle firing at playing cards thirty yards away and hitting the diamond, the heart, as you like; gunslingers with drooping moustaches who acted out famous battles; and tribal chiefs with a pair of feathers on their head, hollow cheeks, and braids down to their legs. I spent two years there, and they were two unforgettable years. But, as someone who really understood animals, I never could forgive Billy for having killed so many bison, some say ten thousand. So one day I decided to leave. The time had come to stop dealing with beasts and start dealing with men. I'd never been frightened of an animal in all my life; I certainly wouldn't be scared of any Americans. In the end it only took me a few years to tame this country, and *that*, boy, is how I became an esteemed west coast impresario and set up my own circus, together with my partner Nathan Goldstein.'

At this point, finally, Mr Gabor turned his cigar in his mouth and inhaled long and deeply. I took advantage of the opportunity to intervene.

'Perhaps you can help me.'

'What kind of advice do you need? Are you a wrangler, a clown, or a tightrope walker?'

'I'm a motion-picture director and I'm looking for information rather than advice: many years ago, I couldn't say how many, maybe twenty or more, a Hungarian equestrienne came to America. The mime Marceline and the juggler Zarmo considered her the most beautiful woman in England. But something happened to her and her career ended.'

'Was her name Eszter?'

'Yes!'

'If she's the one you're looking for, I had a friend called Eszter who had worked for the best European circuses in those years: Herzi, Nagy, Richter... An acrobat who performed on horses. Her act would take your breath away.'

'Yes, that certainly sounds like her.'

'Like me, Eszter left Hungary behind to go flush out fortune elsewhere. She was hugely successful in Britain, as you know, then she too was tempted by America. But things went poorly for her here...'

'What happened?'

'I heard that she had an accident in Youngstown, Ohio. She fell from her saddle during a vault and the horse's hoof crushed her leg. I'd always had the impression that that woman's bones were made of glass, if you follow me. She was crippled for life and couldn't leave town when the circus moved on. Many, many times I've been about to go and visit her...'

'Visit her where?'

'In Youngstown. I believe she opened a flower shop.'

His cigar had burned down a centimetre or two.

'Thank you, Mr Gabor, meeting you has been most useful to me.'

'Think nothing of it, boy, stop by whenever you want and we'll have a chat.' And he wished me good luck.

The next day, with my temples pounding, I returned to Mutoscope. Without stopping to say hello to anyone, I headed straight for the office of Mr Fritz. I climbed the stairs three at a time. As always, I found the boss in his tower seated at his desk and staring out.

'Mr Fritz,' I declared. 'I give up: I'll never find the man who invented the cinema.'

He did not so much as turn in his chair.

'Forget what I told you. And let me get back to my job.'

'As a director?'

'I haven't managed to bring off much else, so far.'

'The MPPC has got us against the ropes, Chas. The hearing date is set for less than two months away. And we don't have any way of getting out of it. I can already hear my mother saying, "I told you so…"'

'Your mother is wrong.'

'In general, maybe, but not where I'm concerned. I've never managed to bring off anything else in this life either. And now I've invested everything I had in the cinema. I thought I was leaping ahead, Chas, and instead I'm still a spoiled and unlucky boy. It's a shame, because our pictures were beginning to sell well.'

'So what do we do?'

'I'm giving you another month.'

'It's pointless, Mr Fritz.'

'You'd prefer to be fired immediately? Surely you found something these last few days, a trail, a clue. Did you work on it or did you stay in bed all week?'

I gave a resigned sigh.

'Make something up, Chas. You're the only one here with the imagination to do it. Even some tiny pretext. I don't need much. Just to win some time in court.'

The man was making me angry. So tied to his illusions that he refused to understand.

'Does this seem like a trail worth following to you: a crippled Hungarian equestrienne who may or may not still be alive and some bloke who used to feed the elephants that I saw once when I was a child?'

It was strange. I'd suddenly been beset by the same irrational despair that Stutters Grogan knew so well, until I taught him how to block it.

'*Gott erhalte, Gott beschütze…*'

'This is no time to start singing, Mr Fritz…'

'*Unsern Kaiser, unser Land!*'

'Please…'

'*Mächtig durch des Glaubens Stütze, Führt er uns mit weiser Hand!*'

'What is that?' The man seemed mad.

'The hymn of the Austro-Hungarian Empire, Chas. The music is by Joseph Haydn. I studied opera singing for many years – in fact the real reason behind my mother's hostility towards the cinematograph is that she never forgave me for not becoming a famous tenor…'

'What do you want me to do, Mr Fritz?'

'*Gut und Blut für unsern Kaiser…*'

'The only thing I know is the city she lived in,' I said.

'*Gut und Blut fürs Vaterland!*'

'It's at least two thousand miles from here.'

'I'll give you sixteen dollars a weeks plus expenses, Chas.'

'It would be like throwing the money out the window.'

'One more reason for my mother to hate me… So, where shall I book this ticket for?'

'For Youngstown, Ohio.'

'Go home, then, and pack your bags, I'm putting you on the first train headed in that direction. Do you at least know her name?'

'Eszter.'

'It's a start.'

'It could be a false trail.'

'Follow it, to the ends of earth.'

'You're crazy, Mr Fritz.'

'No less than you. *Gottes Sonne strahl in Frieden Auf ein glucklich Österreich*, Mr Chaplin!'

A few hours later I was travelling towards Salt Lake City, on a Union Pacific train. From Ogden we would set out for Omaha, Nebraska, on the legendary First Transcontinental Railroad; from there I would continue to Chicago, then all the way to Youngstown.

That morning, at Los Angeles Station, the smoke of the locomotive blackened the air. I looked at the clock, up high on the great white tower. It said six. There were already plenty of people waiting for trains. Commuters, commercial travellers, the usual slice of sleepy and lost humanity you find sitting on benches in stations all over the world. I asked for information from a man in overalls who was dragging some crates of milk bottles. He pointed to a platform where there was a stationary train. The locomotive was black, shiny, with a number beneath the bell:

7108

How many useless details we remember in our lives.

I climbed aboard the last carriage, stowed my luggage, and took a place next to the window. A bit later, a man my size with round eyeglasses and a black moustache entered and sat down nearby, then a woman with red hair. I greeted them with a vague gesture. At the appointed time, with a lurch, the train set off.

'Are you also travelling north, sir?' the man with the moustache asked me.

'More or less,' I replied.

'And you, miss?'

'I'm going to Denver,' said the woman with red hair.

'We may as well get to know each other, seeing as how we'll be spending the next few days together. My name is Joe.'

'A pleasure to meet you,' I said listlessly, 'I'm Charlie.'

I didn't much feel like talking – on trains I always avoided company – but the man did not stop.

'And you?'

'My name is Victoria. Victoria Silk. But you can call me Vicky, if you like.'

Nor was Vicky a woman of few words.

'Happy to know you, Vicky,' said the man with the moustache, ceremoniously shaking her hand. 'Actually, my name's not spelled "Joe", in the American way, either, and I've never been Joseph. My name is G-I-O, short for *Giobba*, *Giobba Formi*.'

'Job? Are you Jewish?'

'No, not *Giobbe*, even if I do have plenty of patience. It's *Giobba*, miss, and I'm not Jewish.'

'I've never heard of a name like that,' said Vicky.

'That's because it's made up! You see, as soon as I arrived in America from Italy, the first thing I learned was how to ask for work. I went to anybody who could offer me something and said to him the only three words I knew in English: *Job for me*. Job for me. Job for me. I've had to change jobs so often that I've repeated those words till I'm sick of them, with my poor pronunciation... so many times that soon, for my fellow Italians, I became *Giobba Formi*. The baker of the neighbourhood where I lived would watch me coming up the street and would say to the others: here comes *Giobba Formi*. And so the newsagent, the newspaper boy, the boiler men, they'd all laugh, "Hey Giobba, no work today, huh?"'

Vicky laughed too. I didn't want to encourage him but the man was beginning to win me over as well.

'What can you do? At this point I'm used to it. I don't even remember my real name any more. But now it's different, I'm engaged. To a girl named Mary. She lives in Nebraska. It's the middle of America and nobody knows me there. Her father has a lumber company, I'll work with them. We're to be married in September. And you, Charlie, by your looks I'd say you weren't born in America either...'

'I was born in a gypsy caravan in England,' I said.

They both laughed.

'You're a funny guy,' said Vicky.

I quickly changed the subject.

'So you're going north to get married, Giò?'

'To get married and to work. Whoever gave me the name *Job-for-me* the first time wasn't wrong. It's my destiny to look for work.'

'It's everyone's destiny, sooner or later. And you?' I asked Vicky.

'I'm going to Denver because I want to write for a newspaper and I've got a friend there who can help me. You wouldn't by any chance be a big landowner?'

'A landowner, me? No.'

'A baseball champion?'

'I'm hopeless at baseball, unfortunately. I get along better with hockey and track.'

'A winemaker?'

'You're getting colder.'

'A gold prospector getting a late start, then?' challenged Vicky.

'In a certain sense. I'm sure you'll go far in journalism.'

'If you need someone to help you dig…' Giò chipped in.

'Sorry, Giò, I've got a different kind of job, though I'm on my way to losing it.'

'Hmm, if you need someone to lose it for you before then, I'm a specialist in the field.'

'I have a better chance of stumbling across a fourteen-carat nugget than of finding the person who would enable me to keep my job.'

The train continued to speed along.

'Is the person you're trying to find a woman?' said Vicky.

I didn't answer her.

For a while we didn't speak.

Endless fields of corn stubble flanked the railway. Then came miles of dusty prairieland. Giò fidgeted nervously on his seat. He began to chat with a passenger seated on the other side of the aisle, a fellow with a hoarse but irresistibly effusive voice. In a few hours the entire carriage knew all about him. His name was Ted and he was a travelling sales-man from New Mexico. The youngest of triplets, he said proudly. He was going to Wyoming to close his latest con-tract, for a consignment of cinnamon-scented soap bars. He pulled one out and had Giò smell it. A sweetish smell spread through the coach, reminding me of my mother's apple pies. Ted had a limitless capacity to come up with one argument after another in support of the benefits of his product. He could have sold anything to anyone – he won over his clients by exhausting them. But I must admit that a great desire to possess that soap came over me as well, and if I didn't buy a bar it was only because the money Mr Fritz had given me was not after all very much.

Vicky tried to sleep, apparently not bothered by all the chatter from Giò and Ted; only the smell of cinnamon prevented her. I thought about my horseback ballerina and her bones of glass. Who knew, maybe it was possible to see through her beautiful exterior to a greater beauty within? I was anxious. That story really must have got under my skin. At least the words being bandied about the carriage presented no such danger, and had the merit of filling the empty hours of the journey.

On the second day, following an uncomfortable night on those narrow but thankfully uncrowded bench seats, we played at who could spot more waterfowl flying over the lonely white expanse of Utah's Great Salt Lake. As evening came on we spied the spires of the Mormon temple of Salt Lake City in the distance.

'You could get off here,' Ted said to Giò. 'Marry yourself three or four pious missionary girls, rather than hand yourself over to Mary and her father. I've heard they practise polygamy in these parts.'

'You're crazy. If I did that, I'd have to work for three or four families at once. For someone like me, who has trouble holding onto even the measliest job, it wouldn't be such a great deal.'

'I guess so,' said Ted, disappointed. 'Not for you or for them.'

From there until Ogden we were attended by a spectacular wall of snow-capped mountains on the horizon. Ogden seemed a cold and windy city, still stunned, a half-century on, to have been crossed by the first railway to reach from one side of America to the other. Someone crazier than me or Mr Fritz had dreamed of uniting the Atlantic and Pacific coasts, and other people had believed in it, and got to work: miles and miles of iron hammered and re-hammered in the snow, in the desert, across the Sierra, the Rocky Mountains, with the Indian tribes, with the Irish drinking like fish, and the Polish and the Italians dying.

Finally the train made a stop. I got off to stretch my legs.

Before me the empty tracks extended on into the night. I suddenly felt very lonely. Maybe I would have done better never to move, to stay in London for ever, on my island.

My life was like that railway line. A cut in the earth, boundless ambition, a desire for something I couldn't name. I spent almost a week on the rails but was never tired. Lonely, yes, but not tired. The train's movement matched my breathing, took me over. I could have kept travelling for ever, never getting off. Circling the earth again and again.

Time in our carriage passed as slowly as the Wyoming landscape. At night each of us stretched out as best we could and tried to block out the noise. During the day we played cards. Rummy, then poker. Vicky read the first chapters of a sentimental novel out loud to us. Ted spoke for a day and a half straight about his two twin brothers and bet us that he would succeed in selling his entire supply of soap bars before arriving at his destination. Giò told stories from his childhood, about the boarding school he attended run by priests; the mountains he saw through the window reminded him of the mountains from where he was from in Italy. I listed all the things that had yet to be invented: a vacuum cleaner to suck up sadness and bad moods; a blender to mix up ideas when we're stuck; a bucket of kerosene capable of wiping out all the wrong things we say...

Station by station, the train eventually reached the city of Green River.

The first to get off was Ted.

'Guys, I'm afraid I've lost the bet,' he said, showing us a suitcase still full of merchandise. 'I owe you a lunch.'

'All the same, it seems to me you've done a good bit of business,' said Giò.

'It could have gone better.'

'Don't complain, before long every woman in Wyoming will be smelling like cinnamon,' said Vicky.

'Hmm, I'm not so sure.'

'What do you mean?'

'I haven't sold a single bar of soap.'

'How is that possible?'

'That's just how it went. There isn't really any contract for me to sign.'

We all remained silent.

'I'll get one.'

'Of course you will,' I said.

He scampered away on his skinny legs, wishing us luck as well.

A few hours later, in Cheyenne, it was Vicky's turn to leave us. There she would catch the line that would take her to Denver.

'I'll be reading you, Vicky. When I see the initials V. S. in the *Denver Post* I'll know who it is.'

'I'm sorry, Charlie.'

'Sorry for what?'

'I've misled you all as well,' she said, rising lithely from her seat. 'I'm going to work as a waitress: my cousin has a lunch-eonette in Denver.'

Her hair was even redder than the hair of the actress who had played Peggotty.

'I'll come visit you soon, then, to see how good the food is,' said Giò.

'Okay. We'll meet there, it's a date.'

'In any case, the meal's on Ted.'

'That's right, it's on Ted. See you soon, then.'

Vicky moved away with a forced smile. She remained on the platform waving until the train pulled out. Giò lowered the blind. He continued to travel with me for another two days. But he no longer had any desire to chat. And silence, from a cheerful type like him, sounded painfully like dissonance.

'Charlie,' he said on the last evening, 'there's no need for me to reach my destination before confessing to you that Mary doesn't exist.'

'And the lumber mill?'

'Nope. All I know is that a new mineral has been discovered in the area, and that there's so much work you don't even need to look for it.'

'Come to Chicago, Giò…'

'No, thank you, Charlie, no job I've ever had has lasted. I told you, I feel like Nebraska is the right place for me. A new beginning – that's what I'm looking for. And there's no better place to hide from bad luck than down a mine.'

At Lincoln station we embraced silently.

'It's a shame,' said Giò, 'it would have been better never to get off this train, since we all know what's waiting for us.'

Left alone in my seat, I pressed my nose against the window until I saw him disappear in the distance.

The next stop would be mine.

Omaha.

The beginning or the end of the First Transcontinental Railroad, depending on how you turn the map. From there, another train would take me to Chicago.

That final train passed through countryside that alternated rows of dead trees against a grey sky and smoking chimneys all the way to the horizon. A Trappist monk sat down beside me. Given my track record, I was afraid even he would want to embark on a discussion, so I kept my eyes lowered; God is a topic in which I have no interest. When the conductor announced the last station, people scrambled to pull down their bags, children to leap and shout, women to plant extravagant hats on their heads. All the vitality that had been repressed for days on end streamed out, like water from an unkinked hose. The monk and I emerged miraculously unscathed, only to be greeted by a violent gust of wind the moment we set foot on the platform. It raised the monk's habit, revealing bare feet in sandals; it caused me to lose my balance and sent a tremor of cold through my bones.

I passed into the crowd. On the platform next to ours another train was pulling out, bound for New York. The people at the windows seemed completely carefree. It was a luxury train, with an imposing locomotive. I envied the man who had designed it. Now there's a truly appealing job, I thought, designing locomotives. I'd have to tell Giò about it, the next time.

The station greeted me in all its majesty: the four enormous white columns framing the exit made me feel smaller than an ant. But I was accustomed to it. I believe that my height has influenced my view of things. From my perspective, the world and other humans always seem entirely immeasurable and inaccessible. And yet.

Chicago was not at that time the rational and boundless city it would later become. But the shape it would take was already there in the streets, where you could breathe in the vigour and industry. The parks on Lake Michigan referred to other, future parks, as did the boulevards to other boulevards, the bridges on the Chicago River to other bridges. Right then, anyone who tried to imagine it could easily see Chicago as it would later be. This too reminded me of the railway that from Omaha had made it all the way to Sacramento, and of the men who had dreamed it before carrying it out.

Perhaps I too ought to have forced myself to dream. To dream the circus drudge capable of inventing the cinema before the Lumière brothers, and an equestrian acrobat with a damaged leg. It seemed as though that was the only way I would get to meet Eszter: to dream her living in an American house, where she would tell me the whole story over a cup of black or cinnamon tea.

I took a room for two nights on the north bank of the river where it flows into Lake Michigan. It was a small, unpretentious hotel, with a middle-aged woman at the front desk. I asked her the price and she told me. The woman adjusted her blonde swept-back hair, and handed me a pen. I signed the registry, paid a deposit, and took my key. First floor, last room on the left. I needed a rest. I climbed the stairs and closed the door behind me, opened the window and looked out. A blue sliver of lake was visible at the end of the road. I took several slow breaths, then closed the shutters and stretched out on the bed. It seemed like a century since I had last touched a mattress. Every bone in my body ached. I slipped my hand beneath the pillow and fell asleep.

I woke up the next day, at lunchtime. I spent the afternoon wandering the city. In one shop I flipped through a magazine.

Production companies were looking for directors. There were ads everywhere. Maybe they weren't worried there about the Motion Picture Patents Company or the Latham loop. I'd heard that Chicago producers had invested a lot of money in the cinema and that they were beginning to compete with Los Angeles. I began to think. Maybe I could try my luck here too. Now I actually had some references, there was a real risk I'd be hired. I liked the city immediately. A new beginning, like Giò said. It's just what we both needed, all it took was choosing the right place. Mr Fritz was already getting along without me in any case. It was no tragedy if I didn't return. Sooner or later I would even be able to send him back the money for my expenses…

I turned it over in my mind all evening. I'd taken down a few addresses where I could present myself. Still unresolved, I closed my suitcase and gave the decision over to a coin. If it came up heads, I would stay in Chicago. I tossed the coin, but I didn't pick it up. I left it there on the hotel floor. The next day my feet woke up curious and refreshed and ready on their own account to leave for Youngstown. Just a moment to talk with the women at the front desk, and I'd be off.

I went back to the station and entered the information office. Five or six men sat behind three long tables covered with stamps and seals and paperwork, schedules and thick volumes, over which electric light bulbs hung down on long cords from the ceiling. On the walls were two maps of the entire United States railway network and a calendar with gigantic numbers. I asked what was the fastest way to get to Youngstown.

'Why do you want to go down there?' said a clerk in vest and tie without lifting his head.

'I have to take care of something,' I replied foolishly.

'You haven't got some girl pregnant, have you?' said the youngest of the group. He had a frighteningly white forehead.

'I would simply like to know which train I need to take to Youngstown.'

'Ah, that's not something you should be asking us,' said a third clerk, he too in a waistcoat, with a jacket and round eyeglasses. 'Try talking to the supervisor, he's the one who knows everything. Maybe he'll also give you some advice about how to handle the situation with that girl.'

I bit my tongue and played along.

'Where can I find this supervisor?'

I wanted to give him a chance.

'Certainly not here. You could try telephoning Philadelphia or Washington, but he's sure to be busy at this hour. If I were you I'd look for a ride in a livestock car. What do you say, colleagues?'

'Sure. There's a hog train leaving soon from platform four. Maybe there's room.'

They were rather enjoying themselves.

I walked up to the first table, picked up a stamp, pressed it down good and hard on the ink pad and before anyone knew what was going on applied it to the youngest clerk's forehead, the whitest I'd ever seen on a man, just like a pristine sheet of paper.

'On behalf of all customers, heartfelt thanks,' I said. And made my exit an instant before a rain of inkwells, pipes, and rulers were unleashed against me.

158

To avoid further trouble I leapt on the first train leaving. I felt better than I had in a long time: I had just discovered the prodigious, even magical power of stamping a man's forehead. I'd been lucky as well. The employees of the Chicago and North Western Railway had involuntarily done their duty and put me on a train running in the right direction, more or less. It was bound for Pittsburgh, Pennsylvania, but I would be getting off before that.

Interior, Night.
24 December 1975

The Tramp is sitting in the centre of the room.

He jiggles a leg, as if he hears music. He rocks his head. Then he rises, asks a row of empty seats if any young lady would like to dance with him. He removes his hat and takes the air by the hand. He clasps its waist and begins to waltz.

He turns away from the hooded figure. Every so often he pulls up the back of his trousers with his cane. Eventually he slips the handle into a belt loop and holds the cane up along his arm. Then he leaves his imaginary partner and continues alone, spreading his arms like a bird.

Once finished he picks up his violin and invites Death to dance. Death shakes his head.

DEATH: You're supposed to make me laugh, Tramp, not dance.

The Tramp slaps his head, as if he had forgotten about their wager. The bowler hat is knocked aslant. He shoos away some pest at his feet, a dog perhaps, a cat or a child, then smiles

broadly as a leg disappears from his trousers, as in a conjurer's
trick.

CHARLIE: Come over here and I'll teach you…
DEATH: What is it you want to teach?
CHARLIE: How to do it. To make a leg disappear,
           I mean… Watch.

The Tramp begins to sing an old song and repeats the movement.
The leg shrinks inside his trousers. Listing to one side, he hops to
the wall and turns around. He lowers himself down on the short
leg, then steps on this foot with the other and straightens up,
stretching the troublesome leg down. He takes something from the
table. Death watches him attentively.

CHARLIE: Here, put these on.
DEATH: What are they?
CHARLIE: Plus fours, old chap, also known as
           knickerbockers.
DEATH: And you expect me to put them on?
CHARLIE: That's right. You need them for the act,
           otherwise it absolutely won't come off.
DEATH: But they're absurd.
CHARLIE: Don't stand on ceremony now…
DEATH: At least turn around. And don't look in the
           mirror.

The Tramp faces the other way. Death removes his black cloak, sits
down, holds the trousers out in front of him, and with great
difficulty threads his feet through.

CHARLIE (*killing time*): You know, when I was little I always
wanted to play the villain.

Death throws the cloak back on his shoulders.

CHARLIE: I would have liked to play you, once...
DEATH: Okay, I'm ready.

The Tramp looks at him. He raises his white eyebrows.

CHARLIE: I've never seen your legs before.
DEATH: That's enough, please...
CHARLIE: Fine, but come closer and give me your hand.

*Death warily extends his hand. The Tramp clasps it in
his own.*

CHARLIE: All you have to do is dangle your leg at the knee
and pull it towards you, like so.

Death imitates him. He's a bit clumsy but makes the effort.

CHARLIE: No, not like that.
DEATH: I don't understand how you do it.
CHARLIE: Try to sing, it will help.
DEATH: I'm tone-deaf.
CHARLIE: It doesn't matter, try. *Señora palafima, voulez-vous
le taximeter, la zionta sur le tita, tu le tu le tu
le wa...*
DEATH: But it doesn't make any sense.

162

CHARLIE: That's not important, come on, repeat after me:
           Tu le tu le tu le wa...
DEATH (*in a shred of a voice*): *Tu le tu le tu le wa...*
CHARLIE: No, I give up, from such crooked wood no
           straight thing can be made!
DEATH: Please, let me try again.
CHARLIE: No, I'm sorry.
DEATH: One last time.
CHARLIE: Do this exercise then: try to grab your ankle.

*Death reaches his skeletal fingers towards his heel. The Tramp
helps him. He lifts a leg as well and stretches it out slightly. In the
exertion his belly slips out of his jacket. A singlet is visible beneath
his unbuttoned shirt. For a few seconds, the two remain balanced on
a single foot apiece, holding on to each other by the shoulder. Then
a dry crack and the hooded figure is left holding his own tibia.
Immobile, he and the Tramp stare at themselves in the mirror
without the least reaction, as if watching a sunset over the
Golden Gate.*

CHARLIE: That's us cut down to size...
DEATH: To the bone.

Death turns towards the Tramp and bursts into shameless laughter.

FIFTH REEL

I completed the last leg of the journey, between Akron and Youngstown, thanks to a series of lucky breaks. First I was picked up by a fabric wholesaler coming from Cleveland. He saw me walking, as I'm wont to, along the edge of Akron's wide high street, as one trolley car after another rushed down the middle. A voice called me over and I didn't think twice. 'Say, I could use a ride in the direction of Youngstown,' I told him. A brawny arm was extended my way and I climbed up into the truck.

A few miles later, in open country, we slowed down as we approached an enormous shed. It might have been one of Henry's warehouses where we shot interiors. Or a hay depot for the animals in Mr Goldstein's circus.

'If you've got a bit of time, my boy, it's worth stopping off here,' the driver said. 'I'll show you something.'

I agreed.

The man was fat and moved slowly ahead of me. He arrived at a fence and called over a young man who was sitting on a metal petrol can.

'Jeremiah, open up, I've got a visitor here. Let's show him our marvel.'

'Where are you from?' Jeremiah asked as he approached.

'California,' I said, 'Los Angeles. I've been on the road for a week and a half.'

'Oh, swell, then follow me. I don't know if anything like this has ever been seen in your parts.'

The fabric man gave a satisfied laugh. He probably brought everyone who passed through the state here.

'I can't resist,' he said. 'When I take this road I always stop here. Puts me in a good mood every time.'

I began to get curious. Jeremiah pushed open a large wooden door and waved me in. The sun blazed into the shed, cutting diagonally across the floorboards and sending the shadows into retreat. When all the surrounding space was illuminated I made out the strange object before me. It was a balloon. A long, grey, cigar-shaped balloon with AKRON written along its side. It might have resembled a circus tent if it hadn't been floating above the ground. Only a number of thick ropes prevented it from resting on the ceiling. Hanging from its belly was a small white cabin; extending either side of its tail were two small wings.

'It's called an "airship",' said Jeremiah. 'There's a factory near here, Goodyear, that would like to mass-produce them. For now we're testing them out. I know they're negotiating with a German company.'

'It's the future, son, don't you think?' said the fabric man.

I was stunned.

'How does it work?' I asked.

'Gas, son, gas and hot air. It's the next step in the evolution of the hot-air balloon.'

'How much gas does it take to raise such a big balloon?'

'A lot. But it's all simpler than you think. Say, we're taking her out for a spin this afternoon – are you up for it?'

'Is it safe?'

'Two of them burned up last week, but never with people aboard.'

'Didn't you say you were looking for a ride?' said the fabric man.

'Where do you need to go?' asked Jeremiah.

I slowly drew out the name: 'Youngstown.'

'We'll take you there, no problem. Are you meeting someone?'

'You could say that.'

'A woman?'

'…'

'Then that's perfect. Just imagine the impression you'll make!'

Over a plank in front of the hangar Jeremiah offered me lunch, cured ham and onions on a slice of bread. As we were finishing up a crew of four arrived.

'We have a passenger,' Jeremiah told them. He had a gap between his two front teeth that was only noticeable when he laughed. The crew member who appeared to be the captain gave me the once-over.

'You look a little pale. Not scared, are you?'

I denied this as strongly as I could manage.

'He's meeting someone in Youngstown,' announced Jeremiah to all present.

'All right then, let's get this big bad bird ready to fly,' said the captain.

Jeremiah and the other men entered the shed and began to apply themselves to a series of ratchet levers. A short while later, with a frightful noise of pulleys and springs, the roof opened up. The captain asked me to take my place in the little cabin beneath the belly of the giant beast. The last thing I saw before the hatch closed was the gap-toothed smile of Jeremiah wishing me bon voyage. I chose a seat in the back and slumped down without speaking.

The airship AKRON lifted off.

I had never flown in my life before, and I've never liked it since. That afternoon I travelled on one of the first dirigibles to appear in the United States. At the beginning I felt nauseous, my head spun and I was scared to look down. But I've never been afraid of heights – once, in New York, I even looked out from the terrace of a skyscraper – and, after a while, I very cautiously moved closer to the little window. The airship had already risen several yards and was now bobbing gently in the air. Occasionally the wind would give the cabin a good shake, but the trip as a whole was rather calm. The captain decided that I deserved a tour of the entire area. First he flew us over the city of Akron, the aircraft's namesake. Seen from above, with its dark roofs, its steeples and smokestacks that blackened the sky, the city seemed to me intolerably grey. We veered across its orderly grid of streets and headed for the open countryside. From up there it was possible to discern the precise outlines of every single plot of land. We crossed over a group of small lakes surrounded by houses, then began to follow the curves of a river; I could make out the trees along the banks, the fishermen, the frog hunters. For a stretch the land was dry and sandy, appearing rusty; other parts were covered with vegetation or factories. The trip carried on like this for a while, then suddenly the captain said something from the cockpit. I failed to grasp the meaning of his words. A couple of minutes later I was approached by another crew member.

'Are you ready?'

'For what?'

'We're almost there.'

I looked down. A group of houses, a few buildings more than ten stories tall, a central square and a high street like so many other American small towns in the depths of the Midwest, with the Stars and Stripes waving over the bank.

'Get ready, you're getting off soon.'

I had no idea what he meant, but I understood soon enough. The airship began to circle like a bird coming in for a landing on his chosen branch, dropping lower at each turn. I felt a strong pain in the pit of my stomach. The captain spied a suitable open space and told his men to ready the counterweights. Without knowing how, without remembering anything, half an hour later I'd been dropped off and was walking alone along the Mahoning River with my suitcase, watching the dirigible's tail disappear into the sky.

I have to admit that as arrivals go, after more than a week of travel on trains, trucks, and air balloons, this one was pretty theatrical. Shame there weren't any clowns or a passing gypsy around to catch the performance, just a few vagabonds strolling along the near side of the river, who cast their gaze my way. Two more lay in the grass drinking. They took turns pouring beer down their throats, then tossed the bottle into the water. They watched me silently.

'You work in coal or steel?' the fatter one called out to me.

He had a strange accent and thickened speech.

'In neither,' I replied.

The two looked at each other uncertainly.

'What'd you come here for then?'

'There ain't nothing else here but coal and steel, or steel and coal, your choice.'

'I'm looking for a Hungarian woman with bones of glass,' I said.

'Too bad, not a trace of Hungarian beer here,' said the first man, and he began to laugh.

The other man laughed too.

The pair were as drunk as Cossacks. I bowed to them and began walking again.

'Wait, stranger. Here there's folks from all over: Africans, Jews, Greeks, Scots, Irish like us. I even know a Syrian. But Hungarians, no, I don't think so.'

'Thanks anyway,' I shouted, without turning my head. Funny how every time I looked for someone or something I kept running into the Irish.

'Even if you haven't come here to slave away in a factory, you're a poor blighter all the same, you can tell from how you walk,' the second man shouted after me.

I continued on my dusty way and in ten minutes or so found myself in Youngstown at last. The town was to all appearances a quiet one, with wide sidewalks and houses of white or rust-coloured brick. Trolleys clattered down the centre of the high street while along the sides were parked the first motor carriages, which some were already calling automobiles. "Welcome to Yo-Town" one sign read. I took it as a good omen. Further on I came to the tree-lined square that I'd seen from the dirigible and sat down on a bench. Across from me rose the imposing Dollar Bank building. I took stock of my situation.

So, I'd made it this far. Now it was just a matter of hunting down the flower shop of a lame acrobat who had immigrated to Youngstown who knows how many years earlier. It was up to me to get the ball rolling. But here the big game was baseball, not hockey like in England. I wiped my feet on the grass and headed for the pitcher's mound. I couldn't decide between a fast ball or a curve ball. I thought about Walter Johnson, who played for the Washington Senators. He was the best young pitcher out there. One reporter nicknamed him 'The Big Train', his arm was so powerful. I made a fist with one hand and picked my luggage back up with the other.

The air was stifling and my heart had begun to tap out an irregular rhythm. I crossed the square and ventured into a secondary street. My suitcase began to feel heavy. I stopped to check my pulse, then entered the next shop I came upon, a Jewish sweet shop with buckwheat cakes, braided poppy-seed loaves, dried-fruit biscuits, and kosher wines in the window. Behind the counter an old man in an apron greeted customers; his beard came down to his chest and he wore a yarmulke on his head. A few yards further along stood a younger man who could have been his son, all eyebrows, bushy moustache, and round cheeks; he observed me with a certain suspicion.

I cleared my throat and addressed myself to the pair of them.

'Have you lived in this town long?'

Neither man responded.

'I wondered whether you've lived here long and if you would be so kind as to point me to a flower shop.'

As a first pitch it wasn't anything special. At this rate the Los Angeles Angels wouldn't make it far.

'You could try at the cemetery,' said the younger man finally, thickening his eyebrows even further.

'The one I'm looking for must be the oldest in town, or at least one of the oldest, if it still exists.'

'There's none older than the one at the cemetery,' said the old man slowly.

'I don't believe that's the one I'm looking for.'

There was a pause. And then the younger man spoke again.

'Perhaps Makrouhi can help you. She's Armenian, been living here for fifty years.'

'And where…?'

'Just continue on till the end of the neighbourhood and ask. Everyone knows where she lives.'

'Okay, thanks.'

'Think nothing of it, stranger.'

'Good day to you.'

'To you as well. And may you find your florist.'

I was disoriented. In a single hour in this small town in the middle of nowhere, I'd already run into two drunk Irishmen, two orthodox Jews, and I was about to go and find an Armenian. At this point it wouldn't have surprised

174

me if a falconer from Kyrgyzstan had crossed my path on a horse.

I followed the street as far as I could and looked around for someone to ask. There was only a small negro boy playing at tossing bottle caps against a wall, but he pointed to a woman sweeping the doorstep of her home. I approached and asked if I could speak with her. Her hair was still dark and she wore a handkerchief around her head. She looked me over from head to toe with piercing eyes that seemed to carry a threat in them as they studied my suitcase and scruffy, melancholy appearance.

'You looking for a place to sleep?'

'That's right.'

'How much money do you have?'

'Enough to pay for a bed, if you're offering.'

'I've got a roast in the oven, come on in.'

Makrouhi lived in a modest but abundantly furnished flat. From a small cast-iron oven came the pungent smell of burnt meat. She transferred the smoking pan to the table, sprinkled the roast with salt, then handed me a plate and told me to take a seat.

'It's been a long time since I ate with a man.'

Her age might have been infinite, the age of everyone who'd ever come to the New World. I thought she might have been beautiful once.

'I was told that you could help me.'

'It's been a long time since I helped anyone.'

'I'm looking for a woman,' I said and began to eat. She narrowed her eyes. I hurried to swallow my mouthful. 'I mean to say, there's a woman I am trying to find.'

'This isn't a place where it's easy to find people. They try not to be found.'

'From the little I've seen...'

'The men in this town are getting organized.' She leaned towards me. 'They gather at night along the river and burn crosses. They have a ridiculous name for themselves that sounds like a tin can being kicked along the road, the Ku Klux Klan. They put on white robes and go looking for negroes to string up from the nearest tree. But they have it in for people like me as well, and for the Jews, for anyone who isn't a Protestant. If you want my advice, go back where you came from, as soon as possible.'

A shiver ran down my displaced, transplanted spine.

'They'll drive us out in a few years. This town won't be the same any more. They'll set fire to our houses. We'll all burn.'

Her words sounded strange to me and I could not imagine such a scene. I feared I'd found myself subject to the ravings of yet another mentally disturbed individual. I didn't know what to say.

'And you,' she went on, 'what kind of rootless drifter are you? Are you Spanish? Turkish? Lebanese? Egyptian? Or mixed blood? Whatever nationality you are, you won't save yourself without money. With money things change. Money's the only thing that can make you American.'

Her face was altered by the words, and it seemed like she was ready to get stuck into her theme, but I didn't come all this way to talk about races and nations.

'The woman I'm looking for is Hungarian,' I said. 'But that's not the point. Many years ago, I don't know how many exactly, she opened a flower shop in Youngstown.'

I chewed another bite furiously. The meat was tough. And everything I said filled me with shame, as if I were trying to fool the old woman by involving her in what would probably turn out to be a wild goose chase.

Makrouhi got up from the table. She had spindly legs but a lively step. Over at the stove, she removed the grill and began to clean it with a rag. I saw her wipe her mouth. Perhaps I'd offended her without realizing it.

'Okay,' I said, 'I admit it. For all I know, this woman could be dead or have moved to another city or taken off with the first circus to pass through here.'

She turned around. A melancholy light crossed her face.

'Tomorrow I will take you there,' she said, and turned back.

Nothing more, for that evening. Just those six words: Tomorrow I will take you there.

An hour later, stretched out on a coarse wool mattress, I repeated them under my breath. It took me a while to fall asleep.

The next morning Makrouhi woke me up early. She asked if I drank milk. I told her I did. Ginger snaps waited on the table. They were somewhat stale but I dipped them in the milk and ate them all the same. Makrouhi sat down next to me.

'We have to go out of town today, but I don't walk as fast as I once did.'

'We're in no hurry,' I told her.

I might have asked her a good many things, but we remained silent. She wrapped herself in a shawl, then took a wooden walking stick from a corner.

It was windy in the streets. We headed towards the

outskirts of Youngstown, in the opposite direction from which I had arrived. Soon the houses were coming farther apart and after a mile we found ourselves in the open countryside. Makrouhi used her stick to point out a signpost: Oak Hill. We turned there and soon found ourselves following a wooden fence across the grass. Beyond it, the new season had inflamed the leaves of the maple trees. Before we reached the gate, the first tombstones appeared. They were white with rounded tops. The oldest leaned towards the earth as if forgotten.

Makrouhi pushed open the gate and entered the enclosure. All the questions I wanted to ask her had died in my throat. We pressed on until we reached the shade of an oak. Makrouhi stopped in front of a headstone smaller than the others. I had remained a few steps behind. Now I approached and read the inscription:

Eszter Neumann
(Budapest–Youngstown)
Acrobat

'Is she the one you're looking for?' said Makrouhi.

I couldn't take my eyes off the stone. Just that name, above; no date of birth, nor of death.

'Yes,' I said, 'I believe so.'

'Yesterday when you spoke about a Hungarian woman and a flower shop, I immediately thought of her. But part of me still thought it was impossible. Then you mentioned the circus and I knew I wasn't wrong. It's been such a long time since I've come to see her.'

Insects landed on the roots of the oak tree. The day took on a sad music I didn't like. Then Makrouhi did a strange thing. She slowly bent forward, as much as her age permitted, and let the walking stick fall to the ground.

'This is what I always used to do,' she said as she struggled upright. 'I came every week and left her a stick. If the next week it was no longer there, I'd bring another one, and another after that. For a year, I made sure she was never without one. I thought it would help her, because who knows how much walking death calls for. And one of her legs was useless.'

Nostalgia marked Makrouhi's voice in the same way old age had marred her face. Suddenly I felt exhausted. My journey ended there, in that graveyard, in front of that headstone overgrown with grass.

Makrouhi continued to speak, but I felt I could no longer listen.

'In the beginning no one in Youngstown believed her story. They thought she was crazy. Who would believe a cripple who shows up and in a few words of broken English says she's an acrobat? Everyone laughed.'

I was no longer following her words, and I had no desire to. I felt only a great emptiness in my stomach, worse than on the air balloon the day before.

'But she knew her way around flowers. For that, she had talent. She would bind them together quickly, confidently, her grandmother had taught her how. Nobody in Youngstown has ever wrapped up a bunch of roses or orchids better than she did. When I saw that, I suggested she open up a little flower shop with my friend Viola, who was blind and had trouble getting by. Eszter said: "A cripple and a blind woman, excellent!" Nobody would have bet on them, but the idea worked.'

Makrouhi's voice went on, as if from far away.

'One evening she asked me to go with her. We went to the riverbank. She hobbled along the whole way. There was a beautiful moon out that lit up the countryside. At the river's edge she let down her hair, which was as red as the leaves on these trees, and long. She tossed me her walking stick. She had never been without it, until then, at least in front of me. She stood on one leg, like a stork. "And now watch," she said. First she began to leap and spin, making use of only her arms and the one leg, turning cartwheels and somersaults; then she dived into the air and for a few minutes was transformed into a fish darting from surface to surface, a weightless being dancing on light, unburdened by shadows. It was everything you didn't expect to see, an anomaly, an act of disobedience, the highest note of a violin, the pride of someone becoming herself once more in another part of the world, along another river, thousands of miles from where she was born. I understood this, I felt it on my skin, and I would have liked to go down to that riverbank and start to jump around myself, with the same sudden transcendent lightness, but my feet have always been heavy, and my legs weren't worth half of hers. I never did manage to overcome the trials, the disappointments, the regrets in my life, and my laboured breathing chained me to the spot as I watched her then. But still her rebellion did me good; a bit of her joy touched me. Like a balm, it loosened the ropes that bind us to the earth. Then Eszter tied her hair back with a ribbon and returned to her normal, limping self. From that evening on I didn't doubt her any more, or her stories, and in the end I was the one who had the word engraved in stone, because that's what she was, an acrobat, and I wanted the shoemaker and the lawyer buried next to her to know it too.

Unwillingly I looked at the headstones to either side, both more upright than hers: Andy Vargas, *cobbler*, it said on one, and on the other: Hubert Moore, *attorney*. In front of the latter, strewn over the ground, were the remains of a bouquet of cut flowers.

'Our friend Viola, on the other hand, had believed Eszter from the start, blindly. Voices never lie, she would tell me. But she can tell you this herself in person, I'm tired of talking. She doesn't live far from here. Let's go.'

It was an order, delivered with the confidence of someone who has always made decisions for herself and for others. But I had to disobey now.

'I'm sorry, I'm not coming.' Now that my crazy hopes of finding Eszter alive had been crushed, I didn't have the strength for any further adventures.

Makrouhi interrogated me silently.

'Viola is waiting for you,' she said then.

'I'm sorry, it's pointless.'

'She's been waiting for you for many years.'

'What does that mean?'

'Eszter said that a man would come asking about her, sooner or later. She hoped you'd find her one day. Viola and I hoped so too. Once I was romantic, now I'm just old and have crooked feet.'

My heart began to pound again in my chest.

'Come, Viola will tell you everything.'

I followed her without further protest. We left the cemetery at a slow walk, a pace corresponding to Makrouhi's energy. There was no one around, no sound but the wind through the trees, the scrape of our shoes. Now that she no longer had her walking stick, Makrouhi held on to my arm. I could feel the sharp edges of her bones. Life had worn her body down, bit by bit, leaving behind nothing but a few dry twigs, the peel of a squeezed-out lemon. We walked back down the street we had earlier climbed, leaving the hill behind us. Farther down, the life of the town picked back up.

A group of older boys stood outside a general store. They had leaned their bikes against the wall and were smoking. They watched us intently and occasionally kicked at the pebbles littering the pavement.

Makrouhi clutched my arm.

I felt all those looks on me, heard the noise made by our shoes.

One boy stepped away from the group and planted himself in our path. He was tall, with a striped shirt and round hat. His teeth were large, slightly irregular, and stained with nicotine. He spat on the pavement, then touched his hat.

'I've never seen you around here before,' he said to me.

I met his eyes without fear.

'If you've come here to find work at the steel mill, you should know we don't need another lousy worker from out of town. Our prison is full of folks who thought they'd start up a union.'

Makrouhi once again sank her knotty fingers into my arm

and tried to drag me forward. The boy stood aside, eyes flashing.

I didn't want to get the old woman involved; I limited myself to a question.

'What's this neighbourhood called?' I asked Makrouhi in a loud voice.

It was the boy who answered.

'Why do you want to know, Turk?'

'Because I don't want to get lost, when I come back.'

'This is Dan's neighbourhood. Come when you like – I'll be waiting for you.'

'See you soon, Dan,' I said.

'Can't wait, Turk.'

It was an appointment. I would return, without a doubt, as soon as I had the chance. I had a great desire to point my shoes in that direction right away, but instead I continued walking straight ahead, almost out of inertia. I breathed without breathing, as if I were underwater and would soon have to return to the surface, but I would have been incapable of completing a single sentence. I wanted to bring to safety this strange woman I'd only known since the previous evening, or at least what little remained of her that life had not yet used up and death had not yet taken.

'They're chasing us out, I told you,' said Makrouhi after a long silence. By then we were out of range of the boys' hearing and we were coming abreast of a block of workers' housing.

'It never changes. Their grandparents owned slaves. And their parents resented anyone who wasn't from round here. They had it in for Eszter, because she was a foreigner, and lame, too. And because she had lots of negro friends, like Viola. Now the family traditions have been passed down to Dan and his friends.'

As Makrouhi spoke I saw other women coming out of their front doors. Two young girls crossed the street in front of us.

'Once they burned down the flower store. Everything except a vase with seven sunflowers. It was the only thing left unscathed in the middle of all those ashes. It made for a strange scene: seven sunflowers in the smoke, with the stalks drooping a bit but the flowers still open, defiant. When it was all over, Eszter went back in to retrieve it and then headed for downtown with that vase in her hands. She looked like a crippled Madonna in procession.'

I thought that now she too, lopsided and leaning into me, resembled a lame Madonna.

'It's my fault we had trouble. I was wrong to pass through here, but I didn't feel like going all the way around the hill the other way.'

I would have liked to tell Makrouhi that there wasn't anything wrong with that, but I didn't want her to hear my voice still shaking.

'I should've guessed that if they saw you with me they'd take you for an Armenian, or a Turk or a Lebanese. It makes no difference to them. Syrian, Jewish, Italian, African, gypsy… Poor devils like us walk on one side of the street, they walk on the other. They've become organized, like I told you. Meeting up outside town at night, performing bizarre ceremonies, all dressed up in white robes. It's to scare us. Their burning crosses light up the whole countryside. They want to purify America – how ridiculous is that? – drive out all the foreigners, shut us all up in a ghetto…'

My desire to return to Dan grew greater and greater.

'I've spent more than fifty years in this town,' Makrouhi went on. 'I've worked the earth and kneaded bread made of wheat from these fields, and it doesn't matter one bit, it's like I was never here.'

I didn't have the courage to look her in the face.

'The truth is, we all come from miserable places. What's yours?'

'Mine's an island,' I said.

Viola didn't live in Dan's neighbourhood; she lived in the coal neighbourhood. Every morning and every evening, dozens of workers arriving for their shifts made their way to the Valley of the Mines, as they called it.

Viola lived on the ground floor of a building of stone and brick. Out front there was a small bell. Makrouhi asked me to pull the cord. Soon the faint sound of steps could be heard and a voice asking, 'Who is it?'

'It's me, Viola, I have a surprise.'

The door opened slowly. Behind it appeared a smiling young mulatto woman and an old woman blacker than the ebony keys of a piano, leaning on a walking stick.

The young woman looked at me as if I were a ghost, and asked me in. A modest parlour: they insisted I sit in the only armchair and pulled up seats around me. On a shelf I noticed a volume of *The Flora of the North America* by John Torrey, *Philosophia Botanica* by Carl Linnaeus, and one called *De Florum Cultura* by a Jesuit priest.

I grew embarrassed as they continued to look at me without speaking. Finally Makrouhi, having rested enough to catch her breath, made introductions.

'This is Naima, Viola's daughter.'

The mulatto woman smiled at me. She had long hair, full breasts, and a lightweight dress on.

'And this is Viola, the one I told you about.'

She nodded. She was quite a big woman, her lower half enveloped by an immense skirt. Without meaning to, I stared at her half-closed eyelids, and the hollow of her eyes, and felt ashamed.

'And you,' said Viola, 'what is your name?'

'My name is...' I began, but my voice died on my lips.

With an effort, I tried again: 'My name is Charlie Chaplin,' I said, 'but I come on behalf of someone else, of Arlequin.'

I might have used Mr Gabor's name, but the relationship between him and Eszter was not entirely clear to me; I suspected another unhappy love story and concluded it was better to stick to the original track.

I sat back and waited for their reaction.

The three women had again fallen into silence. Then Viola raised a hand; her daughter rose with supreme elegance and went into another room. The sound of drawers being opened and closed followed; finally she returned with an envelope. Naima delivered it into my hands with a kind of deference. Her own hands were gentle, her skin smooth. I took the envelope and placed it on my knees, then turned it over.

Along one side of the envelope was written: For Arlequin.

The first to speak was Viola.

'For more than twenty years we've been wondering if

186

anyone would ever come for that envelope. Eszter told me: "It will be a man blacker than the night, like you." "You're pulling my leg," I said, and she laughed.'

Her voice trembled with emotion. As she spoke she slowly rubbed her open hands on her skirt.

'With Eszter you never knew whether she was speaking seriously or not. Her stories were so incredible, so absurd: emperors and tsars attending her performances, bouquets of flowers every evening, acrobats fighting over her… Her voice was honest, I knew, but even if she were lying, what difference would it have made? Isn't transforming one's youth into a bit of fantastic gossip a fine way to mourn it? Who did it hurt? And yet from the day she arrived in Youngstown, there were always rumours about her, about her accident, her solitude, her past… I'm not interested in the truth, Mr Chaplin, it doesn't seem so important any more. People like us have always got by without it, and that's why I'm not asking you to tell me any more than you've already said. But Makrouhi and I immediately felt solidarity with Eszter and with the strange mocking way she had chosen to defend herself. Imagine the reactions of the gentlemen of Youngstown when she declared that she was the daughter of a famous Hungarian trapeze artist named Sandor Neumann, that she had spent her life in circuses across Europe, that for years hers was one of the most acclaimed acrobat acts in the Austro-Hungarian Empire and the United Kingdom, and that finally she had had a disastrous fall from a horse during her first tour in America… Well, we adored her for her courage. I can't explain it, but for us it was as if her brilliant stories made up for a lot of the humiliations. But it also seemed like Eszter

187

might go to pieces from one moment to the next. The good men of Youngstown, and their ever-devoted wives, didn't understand a thing. At first they laughed about it, then they turned nasty and took to treating her like a madwoman. They shouted vulgar taunts and made it hard for her to get any kind of work. Then Makrouhi had this idea for the flower shop. "What can you lose?" she said to us. "You have this child, you've been abandoned by her father, and you can't see"; and to Eszter: "You, on the other hand, you've just abandoned your world, whatever world it was. There's always some wretch who will buy flowers." It seemed like good advice to us, even if the thing would be difficult. In any case, it's not as if we had much choice. Again and again, they came at night to destroy our plants and break the vases, and threatened us with anonymous letters: NEGROES AND CRIPPLED WHORES OUT OF YO-TOWN. But Eszter never recanted a single word of what she called her version of the facts; on the contrary, she continually added new and more surprising details about her past. Until the day the shop went up in flames.'

I was listening attentively to Viola.

'Eszter swore to herself that she would reopen it at all costs and give back to my daughter what the fire had taken away. She had to work very hard, but she did it. Soon, the other immigrants began to come in, to trust us. When I was able to take up my place again and offer the little help I could, for what it was worth, the shop had returned to how it was. With all the flowers and vases in the window. I touched each thing and started to cry. For a little while they left us alone. They ignored us. But Eszter became more cautious. She began to grow old. Still, one morning I heard her changing into her working clothes in the greenhouse out the back, and I confess I felt envy: even with her ruined leg and at her age, I could imagine the glow of her clear, unblemished skin. Her body drew a line in the air among the roses, and there was something so unbearably sorrowful about it that it made her present to me, even though I couldn't see her. Who knows what she must have been like in an evening gown. A glittering gown in the middle of a circus. My blind eyes, Mr Chaplin, imagined the eyes of the men watching her act. The eyes of kings and lamplighters, of sailors, thieves, and moneylenders, of druggists, drunks, actors, musicians, and soldiers, of lawyers, doctors, farmers, adventurers, blacksmiths, and carpenters, of the heartsick, of priests... Before the fire, Eszter had told us that even the clowns and the impresarios she worked with went crazy for her. There was one quarrel – between the two Bastiani brothers – that went so far they threatened to dissolve the troupe if she didn't choose one of them. Beneath that big top, under all those phosphorescent stars, Eszter rejected both of them. One brother swallowed a sword, cutting his throat; the other sold everything and disappeared.'

Viola interrupted herself at this point and asked me if I needed anything. My throat was dry and I told her I would welcome a glass of water. Her daughter went to get it and once again I had the opportunity to admire the tremendous grace of her movements.

'Then,' Viola continued, 'one morning Hans showed up at our shop. I opened the door, and I'm sure that someone in the street stopped to stare. It must have been quite a peculiar scene for the inhabitants of our little burg: a blind woman and a dwarf standing like statues at the front door. "Does Eszter Neumann work here?" asked Hans in a high voice. He let me touch his head and face and I could feel that he had a mischievous air about him. His eyes took up a large part of his face and he was shorter than an anemone stem. Nobody in Youngstown had ever met a dwarf before. There was Amos, of course, whose body was all crooked and who had to lean on his arms to get around, and Homer, whose mind was addled and who had an extra toe on each foot. But no dwarves, ever. Stupefied, I let him in. Then I quickly closed the door. I was afraid of who else might arrive: a man in a barrel, a snake charmer, a confraternity of monkeys, all the characters in those insane stories. Eszter began to cry as soon as she heard him speak.'

'Perhaps we're boring you?' interrupted Makrouhi. 'There's no need to tell you a story if you already know it.'

'I only know a part of it, Makrouhi. It's vital for me to know the rest.'

Viola looked grateful, as if seeing her account through to the end, out loud, was something she needed to do.

'Please continue,' I said, while Naima poured me more water.

Viola smoothed out her skirt and waited for me to finish drinking before she began to speak again.

'Hans stayed with us for about a week,' she said. 'The language he spoke with Eszter could have been Hungarian or Russian or German, for all I know. I think that he was in love with her too, but Eszter would laugh when I said so. One evening, as we were finishing dinner, Hans cleared his throat and announced that he'd be leaving the next morning. I heard him taking something out of his bag. "This is from Arlequin," he told her. "From Arlequin?" asked Eszter.'

Viola rubbed her hands across her skirt once more.

'Mr Chaplin, I don't know who Arlequin is, I never met him. All I know is what Eszter told us. That he was a giant with enormous shoulders and tiny hands, and that no one had any idea where he came from, though it's obvious the man must have been a bit touched in the head. She told us the circus kept him on because in Europe you didn't often see men with skin so black. The impresarios realised that he was just as astonishing to the public as an exotic animal, like a giraffe or an elephant, and so they used him as an assistant in tons of acts, but it wasn't because he had any special abilities. Is that how it was, Mr Chaplin? He simply handed knives to the knife throwers, poles and harnesses to the tightrope walkers, chairs to the clowns, fed the animals and cleaned up the big tent after the audience had left… Anyway, this Arlequin had given Hans something for Eszter: he was holding a crank-handled box. Eszter asked him what it was, and Hans replied that it was a belated parting gift. On the day Eszter had left for America, all the members of her old circus had given her something. Even the bearded lady gave her a pair of earrings, and everyone had thought she hated her. But Arlequin had given her nothing. And now she had his box. After that she became convinced that Arlequin himself would come. She never stopped waiting for him.'

Viola stopped.

'She waited for Arlequin for years, Mr Chaplin. And we kept on waiting after Eszter died.'

'And now we're happy that you're here,' concluded Makrouhi. 'On behalf of him.'

'Thank you.' I could barely speak.

Naima smiled at me. I stood up.

There was nothing left to add.

Viola extended a hand in my direction.

'From time to time, Makrouhi and I repeat this story to each other to fill up our old age. Forgive us. You've been very patient.'

I looked at her a last time.

'Just one thing,' Viola said then.

Her daughter returned to the other room; I imagined her rummaging through the yellow belly of some ancient chest of drawers. When she reappeared she was carrying a wooden box. She held it out to me.

'You take it, it's of no use to Eszter now. And it's of no use to me. Naima and Makrouhi know well what's inside. Deliver it to Arlequin along with the envelope.'

I said nothing. I picked up my bag and touched her arm.

I returned to Makrouhi's apartment late that evening. I had needed a walk to release all the tension I'd built up. From the coal neighbourhood I went down into the Valley of the Mines and then to the gravelly banks of the river. The Mahoning had gouged the earth like an animal fleeing before a hunter, carving out curve after curve over the entire plain. I followed its winding path for a long stretch, until my legs were tired and my head was empty. When I returned to Youngstown, the light of day was dying.

Makrouhi was waiting for me, sitting on the threshold of her home. She rocked her shoulders back and forth slowly.

'There's something to eat on the table, if you're hungry,' she said.

'I'm leaving tomorrow, Makrouhi.'

'You should eat all the same, you'll need the strength.'

'Thanks, I will.'

On the table I found some cheese and a tomato, and bread in a basket. I took a slice and poured myself a glass of water. When I finished I washed what there was to wash and reset the table. Above the sink, Makrouhi had hung a shelf on the wall, with an old weighing scale, some dried flowers in a glass, a broken vase, and a good number of candles. I dried my hands and went back outside.

Makrouhi was still rocking on her perch, watching the deserted square.

'I'm going to bed,' I said.

I stood for a bit at the door, unsure if I should say anything more. I knew that the next morning she would stay closed in her room until I left. I would have liked to touch her shoulder and stop that incessant motion of hers. It would have been like stopping time, like seizing the pendulum, suddenly bringing all the things that vacillate on the threshold of danger – to rest. Or like reaching out, from across an ocean, to lightly brush the cable-knit cardigan of a mother seated at a window, and bringing her back.

'It's been a lovely day,' I said after a long silence.

'Yes, it's been a lovely day,' repeated Makrouhi.

I only took out Eszter's envelope for Arlequin once I was

in bed. I weighed it in my hands. Then I picked up the wooden box those women had delivered into my hands and set it down in front of me. I sniffed it. It smelled of cherry. I sat the box up on one end. It had two glass lenses near the top of one of the short sides, and a crank on one of the wider sides. I had crossed America and I still didn't know exactly what for.

But still, I hesitated. I didn't have the courage to put my eyes to the box. I was afraid that any magic inside would vanish at a glance. I would show it to Henry and Ricardo as soon as I got back. If the story so far was true, whatever this box contained, it had to have been made a few years before the invention of either the movie cameras patented by the MPPC or Eastman Kodak's flexible roll film. Whatever bizarre contraption it was, a magic lantern or some kind of chronophotographic device, the man who had built it must have been an extraordinary pioneer. With all due respect to the Latham loop.

I put it all away and hastily packed my bags. That madman Mr Fritz could be proud of my work. Everything had unfolded rather more quickly than anyone could have guessed. Back in Los Angeles I would ask him for back pay, my immediate reinstatement as director, and the head of Brandon. That dandified excuse for a gag writer who only ever made jokes at my expense wouldn't have so much to laugh about any more. Now, I just needed to get back in time to prepare the case against the MPPC in the best possible way, in concert with Mr Fritz's lawyers, assuming that he had enough money left to pay them and that his mother hadn't disinherited him. If we pulled it off, they would be talking about this trial from

California to New York, as the greatest counteroffensive in American history against a monopoly in a growing industry. I fell asleep imagining the newspaper headlines:

THE LITTLE ENGLISHMAN WHO DEFIED
THOMAS ALVA EDISON

EPITAPH FOR THE LUMIÈRE BROTHERS

THE MOVING STORY OF THE MOUNTEBANK WHO
INVENTED THE CINEMA OUT OF LOVE

SMALL PRODUCTION COMPANY DISMANTLES
COMMERCIAL MONOPOLY

CHARLES CHAPLIN'S HOME RUN

MPPC: HANDS OFF THE CINEMA...

Some echo of the press campaign would surely reach Europe, and maybe even Arlequin, if he were still alive, if he knew how to read, would sooner or later see an article about himself...

Sleep came easily and was full of dreams.

The next day I woke up full of energy. As I had predicted, the door to Makrouhi's room was closed. She didn't want to see me leave. I was grateful to her for this as well. A single day had been enough for us to become fond of and lose each other. I closed the door and crossed the street.

This time I would make my way without side trips or unscheduled stops. No airships. No discussions with North Western Railway employees. Just one train to catch, the right one. For Omaha, and then from there, retracing my steps, for Ogden, Las Vegas, Salt Lake City...

The train station lay outside the town. I had seen railway tracks the day before, running along the river. Youngstown had brought me luck. It had given me back something that reminded me of my childhood. When Dan's friends appeared from behind a pile of sand, I was whistling a popular tune my father used to sing.

Finally Dan himself appeared; I continued to whistle.

'Hey, Turk, the two of us had an appointment.'

I walked on.

'I don't care for folks with short memories,' Dan said.

He had on the same striped shirt as yesterday. He smiled, revealing his big, dirty, uneven teeth.

I walked past as if I hadn't heard him. Dan caught up with me and put a hand on my chest.

'I don't much like people who whistle neither.'

'I'm following your advice,' I said then with great effort as I moved his hand. 'I'm on my way out of town, so you can rest easy. Even if I'm not Turkish.'

'Too late, midget. If I remember right, yesterday you challenged me in public, and no one challenges Dan McRoy in public and then hooks it. In these parts we call that cowardice. Ain't that right, you Turkey-denying Turk?'

I said nothing.

'All you've got to do is admit it in front of my friends, after that you can even beat it, for all I care.'

'That's a generous offer, Dan,' said one of his friends.

'C'mon now, repeat after us: I am a yellow-bellied coward, a yellow-bellied coward,' said another.

I set down my bag and laid my jacket on top of it, then I rolled up my shirtsleeves.

Dan smiled.

'On your guard,' I said, advancing towards him.

'Hey, guys,' said Dan, 'the mouse has turned into a lion. I really think I better take to my heels.'

His friends laughed ostentatiously.

Dan avoided a jab, showing he had good reflexes, but never even saw the second punch coming. It was a combination I reserved for the biggest occasions. He dropped like a marionette gone slack. I was almost disappointed. I picked up his hat from the sandy ground and tossed it his way.

I had just retrieved my stuff when something slammed into my back. I don't know what hit me, but whatever it was must have been very hard. I fell to my knees. An instant later came a hail of kicks and cudgel blows. Now I too was rolling around in the dust and couldn't do anything but take it. There had to be at least three of them. I tried to protect my bag. I curled myself over it and placed my arms on either side. I thought of nothing but the box inside. I was terrified they would damage it and the thought made me crazy.

Two hours later, a group of workers found me as they returned home from their shift at the mill. One of them said they shouldn't get involved, they should just inform the authorities, but the one who must have been the foreman said that calling the authorities would already be taking a risk. The only choice was between leaving me or helping me. When he began to take off his overalls, no one rebelled. Another man removed his overalls as well and they tied the two pairs together, then settled me inside as if it was a hammock and ordered the other workers to carry me into town, so their women could help me. They tended to my injuries that evening, but many wagered I wouldn't make it through the night. No one knew me from the mill. It didn't matter. The ones who had reduced me to that state always hit their targets. They always had it in for the same unlucky wretches and they always attacked in packs.

At some point, a little boy said that he had seen me the day before leaving the Oak Hill cemetery with the old Armenian woman who lived in Yo-Town, and they sent someone to call on her immediately. By that time, I was delirious. In the middle of the night, Makrouhi had me transported to Viola's house and entrusted me to the care of her daughter, who looked after me from then on. At daybreak I was burning with fever and my body was black and blue and cut up all over, but I was still alive.

It took weeks for me to heal. Days of compresses, ointments, and decoctions of sarsaparilla root and dried elderberries. Days of pain in my bones, nausea, bruises and swollen eyes. Drinking from a straw. Bandages. Bloody, matted hair, a stubbly face, and night fever. Naima treated my silences and my rages, my impatience and my complaints, just as she had done all her life for her mother. She showed me that the bag and its contents were safe, at the foot of the bed. 'Don't worry,' she told me, 'as soon as you're able to stand and rinse your own face you can leave again.' Every night I felt her watching over me in silence.

I resigned myself to the situation; everything else would have to wait. But it was like a truce. I realized that I hadn't spent so much time in bed since I was sick with smallpox as a small boy. Since then, no one had looked after me with such care. My injuries notwithstanding, that month was the first vacation – however absurd the circumstances – that life had imposed on me.

Naima had set me up in a sliver of a room at the back of the house, but I lacked for nothing. From time to time Viola too would come to visit me. I would hear her walking stick tapping the wall. She entertained me by speaking of the medical properties of *Nelumbo nucifera*, commonly known as the lotus flower. Less frequently, Makrouhi stopped by. She would stand behind the chair and watch me sleep.

As soon as I managed to raise myself up a bit on the pillows, I asked Naima for a pen and ink and the notebook I kept in my bag. Naima had no trouble finding it. She also brought me a wooden bookrest I could write on, then she left me alone. Clutching the pen between my fingers was painful, but I forced myself. I opened the notebook and made out a list of things I'd learned and was afraid I'd forget.

A black circus drudge: Arlequin
Eszter: equestrian ballerina
Eszter has bones of glass
Eszter fell and broke her leg
Eszter sells flowers in Youngstown
Eszter's father was a trapeze artist
For love of Eszter, one of the Bastiani brothers
     swallowed a sword, the other disappeared
Arlequin built a magic box to capture time
Some years later, Eszter is visited by a dwarf

Conclusion no. 1: cinema was invented in a tiger's cage

It's the list of a madman, I thought. If that page had fallen into the hands of a doctor, there would be no question about his diagnosis. But seeing my reflections set down on paper reassured me. As if each of those words were lighter than an air balloon and now I had bound them to a mooring mast. Meanwhile, time was passing. My days were numbered, in every sense.

Just as she had promised, forty-eight hours after I rose from bed, Naima accompanied me to the station, together with a group of workers. Just in case. They put me on the first train for Omaha. I saw them disappear on the platform like a bunch of extras from a final frame, the slim figure of Naima at the back. In the train window I caught the reflection of my awkward, broken smile.

I spent the last week of convalescence on the train, sleeping and waiting for strength to return to every single part of my body. My still-aching muscles were spongy and I struggled simply to open and close my hand. It was just a few days before the MPPC trial when I arrived in Los Angeles. I gave all the money I had left to a man with a leather cap pulled low on his head and a black automobile with red-spoked wheels. A Ford Model T. I asked him if he could take me to Tamarind Avenue as fast as possible. He told me to climb in.

The man whom the employees of the Levy Fritz Mutoscope Company saw step down from the car in a cloud of dust at their front gate was a sorry sight. He dragged his feet a bit and leaned on a bamboo cane; his elbow was bandaged, his cheeks still swollen, and his boots worn down like the kind my grandfather used to resole. But his profile should still have looked familiar. And yet no one seemed to recognize me. I started towards the shed where Henry worked. After a few steps everyone had lost interest in me. They had only stopped to look at the black Ford now leaving another dust cloud in its wake. Not exactly a festive welcoming committee. But then no one could have expected my arrival. The first to greet me was Bennet, a film editor who had been rather useful to me on a couple of occasions.

'Hey, Charlie,' he called out.

I went over to him enthusiastically.

'Did you fall off a bicycle, or what?' said Bennet, clapping me painfully on the shoulder. I was about to reply that I'd never learned to ride a bicycle properly, but I was unbeatable on airships. He didn't give me the chance.

'I'll see you around, Charlie, they're waiting for me,' he said hastily and took off for the warehouse where we shot interiors.

As he moved away I observed energy and satisfaction in his every step. I looked up. Everything there gave the impression of being infected with a cheerful hysteria. As if people were no longer wandering about aimlessly, in chaos and insecurity. Carpenters, electricians, technicians... Everyone seemed to know their role. I had no idea what was going on. I headed towards the control tower and climbed the stairs as rapidly as I could manage. Mr Fritz was sitting in his usual spot, sunk in his armchair. His white curls had become a bit longer since I'd left. His desk was strewn with documents and two women bustled in and out of his office continually.

He noticed me only when I had reached his desk and blocked his light. He raised his eyes. His cheeks seemed to me bigger and flabbier as well. He removed his eyeglasses, wiped the sweat with a handkerchief, and broke into a smile.

'Chas, have you met my new secretaries?'

I shook my head, no.

'This is Evelyn, and this is Katie. I'm thinking about having them run the press office.'

'Hi, Chas,' said Evelyn and Katie, in unison.

I greeted them with a nod, then they disappeared into another room.

Mr Fritz returned to his papers.

'Pardon me, Chas, but I've got to read through this file by this afternoon. Quickly, though, tell me, how's life?'

Maybe he was studying the trial briefs.

'I found what we were looking for,' I said in a low voice.

Mr Fritz seemed not to notice.

I repeated the words, enunciating each syllable.

'I found proof, Mr Fritz.'

Mr Fritz raised his eyes from his papers. His expression seemed absent, as though he had no idea of what I was talking about. 'Proof of what, Chas?'

For the past week, on the train, I had shot endless short films in my head. Ones in which, when everything was lost, I arrived to save the day, still covered in bruises, in the same state Dan and his friends had left me, but with laughing eyes. This was why I hadn't sent a telegram ahead. So that I would remain until the very last minute the company's one remaining hope, so that I'd reappear like someone returning from the ends of the earth, bringing reinforcements and lifting the siege on the castle. But among countless possible reactions I'd imagined, Mr Fritz's response was not one I'd expected.

I sensed the annoyance seeping into my voice.

'I've been on the road for weeks, travelling all over America on every form of transportation possible, I've been beaten with sticks beside a river, and you don't remember for what?'

Mr Fritz's face remained unchanged, betraying no hint of curiosity; on the contrary he himself seemed annoyed, as if at an unwelcome interruption.

'You gave me a month's advance, at sixteen dollars a week, to carry this out,' I continued.

Only at this point did his cheeks quiver slightly.

'You've always had a great memory for money, Chas, but I believed that payment was your severance fee. A fine way to get yourself out of trouble, I'll give you that, very original.'

'But I have absolutely no desire to leave the company.'

'I'd placed so many hopes in you, and I have to say I felt betrayed. You were the first to abandon a sinking ship – an example followed by many others, if it's any consolation. Between the actors and technicians who cleared out at the first sign of bankruptcy, we lost a third of our staff, in addition to you, some to Chicago, some to our direct competitors here in LA.'

'You really thought I would sell myself to someone else?'

'I didn't think anything, Chas. I only wanted to wash my hands of the matter, just like you. In the end you deserved the money: up until then, you'd been a good worker.'

'I don't believe this.'

'Let's put it this way, then: I'm a gambler who doesn't know when to quit. I always want to see the cards, and your bluff was so obvious that you needed to be taught a lesson.'

'I needed to be taught a lesson?

'Don't take it badly, Chas. So you bluffed and you lost…
But, honestly, those thirty-two or sixty-four dollars are worth
the price of this spectacle. I knew you'd come back with your
tail between your legs. I would have bet anything. You waited
just long enough for the storm to pass.'

'I don't know what you're talking about.'

'That idiot Brandon – the one who was so quick to get on
your nerves – was right: you chose the wrong career. You're
not cut out to be a director, and not a gag writer either. If this
little routine is the best you can do, you'd have better luck
reading someone else's lines. As an actor. Here, take this, it's
the address of a friend of mine, Mack Sennett. Go to him
and use my name, but no tall tales this time, please.'

No sooner were the words out of his mouth than his flesh
was rocked by a sudden fit of violent laughter. His belly
leaped and shuddered.

'I haven't gone looking for other work, Mr Fritz, and I'm
not acting now.'

'Neither am I. So, what do you want? I don't have time to
waste with deserters like you.'

I bit my tongue. If I hadn't promised myself I'd see this
through to the end, I would have been on my way that very
instant. I reached down into my bag and drew out Arlequin's
box.

'Here, this is the proof I was talking about.'

I set it down on the desk, on top of all his documents.

'I have to say, Chas, you've never lacked for imagination.
And you really don't give up.'

'Just take a look at it.'

'Let it go, Chas. I've appreciated your performance, but now, please, walk out that door and never show yourself here again. And now I've got a headache as well. I'm not asking you to give back a single dollar. Let's say we're even – it's not a bad result for you, believe me.'

'Look inside, Mr Fritz.'

'You are a real pain in the ass, Chas.'

Finally Mr Fritz reached out to touch the box.

'And what would this be?' he asked.

'This is a cinematograph, Mr Fritz, from before the Lumière brothers.'

'Hmm, so you thought you'd spring a surprise finale?. You've got guts, Chas, but we're through. Be off and don't make a fuss.'

'But this box will allow you to win the case, Mr Fritz.'

'If that's what you're on about, as usual your timing's off. The MPPC withdrew its injunction a few days after you left. But don't pretend you don't know this, it's been in all the papers.'

'They withdrew the injunction? So, our company no longer runs any risk, then?'

'*My* company, Chas, mine. No, no court will shut us down. In fact, seeing as how you're so short on news, I can tell you that in the past few weeks our Civil War picture, *The Bluecoats*, has proved such an unexpected hit that all our accounts are back in the black.'

A nauseating drone invaded my ears. I retrieved the box along with the address for Mack Sennett, put them away, then shouldered my bag.

'So, drop the act. What do you really want, Chas?'

asked Mr Fritz from his chair, before I left. 'Is it more money?'

I turned my back on him.

'Well, then, what did you come here for?'

I was a step away from the stairs.

'I want you to believe me, Mr Fritz,' I said without turning around.

I left the building in a state of complete shock, like I was on a bicycle and someone had cut the brakes. Even if I turned the pedals in the opposite direction, it just kept going faster.

Mr Fritz was right about one thing: the time had come for me to put the whole sorry affair behind me and take up my true vocation again.

Interior, Night.
24 December 1976

The Tramp stands before an enormous terrestrial globe.

He examines it greedily. Caresses it. Kisses it. Then lifts it in the air. Spins it on one finger. Tosses it from one hand to the other. Gives it a kick. Catches it, clasps it in his arms, like a Greek statue. Gives it another kick. Lets it roll over his shoulders. Stretches out on a table and begins to juggle it with his behind.

Once, twice.

Slowly.

DEATH: That's enough, Tramp, it's not worth such an effort.

CHARLIE: You're right – like the majority of the men who inhabit it, the world is nothing but a bloated sack of hot air. Here, take it. (*He tosses it at him.*)

Death is caught off guard. He rises from his chair and strikes the rubber globe with a header that nearly causes his hood to slip off. The Tramp, still lying on the table, sends it back with a heel.

DEATH: Does this seem like the moment to start
          playing?

CHARLIE: There's no better way to die, don't you think?

*Death looks at the approaching ball with confusion. He returns it
awkwardly with an elbow.*

CHARLIE: That's it, well done. Let's say that the first to let
          it fall loses.

*The Tramp gets down from the table and sends the globe into the
air again.*

DEATH: No matter how it goes, Tramp, you've already
          lost.

CHARLIE: Now this is why people say you've got a nasty
          character.

DEATH: It's not true, I have the character suited to my
          job.

CHARLIE: You're really in a dark mood tonight…

DEATH: Me? And what about you?

The two continue to juggle the globe.

CHARLIE: What about me?

DEATH: You're the saddest comic actor I've ever seen.
          At the cinema…

CHARLIE: What, you go to the cinema?

DEATH: Sometimes, as necessary. For people who expire
          in a red velvet chair, or on set.

CHARLIE: Why didn't you come to take me while I was shooting a film? What a scene that would have made...

DEATH: You see how sad you are?

CHARLIE: I'm not sad, it's just that I don't want to die now.

DEATH: You're a tragic actor, Tramp. Once I read in a newspaper that the Latin Americans call you Carlitos, *el genio de la desventura*...

CHARLIE: You read the papers as well?

DEATH: The obituaries, of course. It's my entertainment section.

The Tramp thinks about this for a moment, raising one eyebrow.

DEATH: Careful, it's going to fall...

The Tramp suddenly rouses himself and somehow manages to strike the globe before it hits the carpet, but the result is such a wild shot that Death must spin and lunge to reach the ball, sending it further into the room.

DEATH (*looking up from the ground*): At least try for it.

The Tramp sets off at a run, but Death stretches out a leg and trips him. The Tramp tries desperately to maintain his balance and instead begins to reel around the room, flailing his arms and staggering.

CHARLIE (*falling*): Doesn't count!

209

As a boy he was a master tumbler, but this time he's not acting. He clutches at the curtains, knocks into a chair, slams into the wall, but with a final bound reaches the rubber globe and punctures it with a Swiss Army knife that has suddenly appeared in his hands. The ball sputters and darts through the air, uncatchable. Death's cowl follows its convulsive path but the skeletal legs don't know which way to go. The world drops, deflated, at Death's feet.

DEATH: You cheated!

The Tramp shakes his head, unmoved. Death is flabbergasted.

DEATH: This wasn't the arrangement!
CHARLIE *(through his panting)*: Nobody said we couldn't puncture it. And anyway you cheated, too; you lost, and I don't have to make you laugh.

The Tramp aristocratically crosses his left leg over his right and begins to lean back in the chair, but his hand slips on the armrest and he ends up smashing his head against the solid-wood table. The Tramp is knocked senseless, his tongue hanging out. The hooded figure approaches and looks at him: one of the actor's eyes stares out dully like that of a fish on ice, but his gormless grimace puts Death in a good mood.

DEATH: Okay, Carlitos, this year will be my gift to you. You really are the saddest comic actor I've ever seen; you would have made a wonderful Hamlet.

Death places one hand on the Tramp's skull and another on his chin. Then, with a sudden, clean jerk of his hands, he straightens up the Tramp's neck as if it were a marionette's.

Some moments later, the Tramp regains consciousness. The room is empty. Without any clear idea of what has happened, he looks at himself in the mirror and realizes he's still alive.

SIXTH REEL

Before definitively surrendering to my destiny as an actor, I returned once more to England, to visit my mother at the Cane Hill lunatic asylum. When I entered, she continued looking out of the window, as she had always done. Her hair was grey and she was speaking to the chairs, and cursing. She did not turn in my direction but I knew she recognized me all the same. She caressed her velvet jacket. 'If only you had brought me a cup of tea that afternoon,' she said, 'I would have been just fine.' I sat down beside her on the cot. Its frame was silvery grey. We didn't exchange another word.

When Fred Karno saw me walk into his London office again to ask for a part in one of his shows – any part, even a walk-on – I didn't even need to open my mouth. He greeted me with a regal smile and asked me no questions. From a desk drawer he drew a folder with my name on it and handed it over. Inside was a contract to be the company's leading man. I was waiting for you, he said only, chewing on the end of his cigar. I signed without reading it and a week later I was already en route to a new theatrical tour overseas. I was no longer afraid to take the stage. I crossed America all over again, and a few months later I arrived back in Los Angeles. We were performing *A Night in an English Music Hall*. I played the part of the old drunken dandy, the same one I'll play this evening, for an audience of one, as soon as I've finished writing this letter. The theatre rocked with laughter without knowing that it was applauding the son of an alcoholic and I enjoyed such a resounding personal success that the other members of the company became envious. When the show closed, they gave me a tobacco box wrapped in tin foil and filled with bits of dried greasepaint. With a card: *A bit of shit for a shit.* I had just bought a round of drinks for everybody. I took it so badly that I decided to go my own way, this time for good. In my pocket I still had the address for Mack Sennett that Mr Fritz had given me and I decided to give it a try.

The next day I found myself before a man with two colossal black caterpillars in place of eyebrows, a square jaw, and a full mouth. Uncultured, but with infectious, irresistible enthusiasm for everything he liked. 'You're too young for the cinema,' Sennett told me during that first meeting. 'I can grow as old as you like.' The joke pleased him. He gave me a loud slap on the back and signed me up for a trial.

That rainy afternoon in 1914, as I searched the men's dressing room at Keystone Studios for a costume for a scene we were shooting, I had uppermost in my mind what Fred Karno had told me, that all stories can use a pinch of melancholy. It wasn't hard for me to find it: I already carried it in my eyes, in my hands, in my blood. To go by what women say, I had a bit of sadness in my loins as well, but this always proved a source of fascination for them. I thought that if I

216

could put a grain of this melancholy into a comedy, I might well be able to seduce anyone. The trick was to upset the common sense of proportion. So I chose a pair of shapeless trousers, struggled to button up a vest and jacket that were too tight, and put on two enormous, worn-out shoes. I looked at myself in the mirror. I'd never felt so at ease. My outfit was an act of disobedience. I mussed my hair and added a bowler hat, a cane, a bow tie. Just one final detail was missing. I stuck a narrow black moustache beneath my nose and for the first time in my life, I recognized my own face.

When I emerged from the make-up room in that wretched get-up and stood in front of the camera with that wolf Mack Sennett watching, all I had to do was to move as if I had fleas under my arms. Sennett began to laugh in such an exaggerated, hysterical manner that he started to cough; tears came to his eyes and he very nearly choked. I had him in the palm of my hand. I whirled the cane under my nose as Marceline had taught me and scuttled away with my feet flapping and a nervous air, imitating the manner of the old London coachman my mother and I used to spy on every evening from our garret on Pownall Terrace. It felt as though I was skating on a single leg or standing on the edge of the Grand Canyon. I wiggled my moustache and winked at all the women present, but my hands were shaking. For ten minutes I did nothing but stumble after every skirt that passed by; then I entered the set of a hotel lobby with the air of a vacationing millionaire, but furtively stole candy from a child, took a swig from a flask, and apologized to a spittoon I'd bumped into...

When I grabbed a dog by the tail and ended up head over

heels on the floor, it wasn't just Sennett who was laughing but also the stagehands, the cleaning women, the builders, the extras. They weren't laughing at what was happening, for all that it might be comic or absurd; they were laughing at me, at the way my face registered every little thing, at my terrible incompatibility with the world. Because if you're truly ridiculous, the costume doesn't matter.

They kept on laughing for years, without the power to stop, and I signed contract after contract, until I became the highest-paid actor of all time: $670,000 a year, more than $10,000 a week. It didn't take me long to make so much money that I could build my own studios just two miles from Mr Fritz's, on a five-acre lot covered with orange trees. I even acquired a blue Locomobile with white tyres, and hired a Japanese driver named Kono. The evenings when I'd stood outside gazing into the restaurants on Carson Street were light years away; now I could dine every day at the Armstrong Carlton Café, at Musso's, or anywhere on Hollywood Boulevard I wanted. Salmon, smoked herring, sheep's heart, or kidney pie.

From that moment on, cinema absorbed all my energies. I had the patience of a mule, capable of repeating the same scene a hundred times over. Some nights they had to put me to bed with my make-up still on, because I would never have stopped. To keep in shape, I exercised in the gym or swam in the pool before dinner; earlier in the day I would get a manicure and pedicure – I've always had a great devotion to my hands and feet. By now I was following a strict regime: I never played cards, drank nothing more than a small glass of port from time to time, and then only so my new colleagues wouldn't think me a sombre, teetotalling monk like the actors in Karno's company had believed.

Only on Tuesdays would I distract myself with boxing matches at Doyle's, just south of LA in Vernon. One night I happened to see Stutters Grogan win hands down against a Texan. He was still the best, in my eyes, and he remembered all the fakes I had taught him. Webster was there, too. He spent the whole time behind the ropes, down on his knees, his hair gone white. But I didn't enter the locker room. I walked away from them and from the crowded arena, just as I had done in San Francisco, with the same prayer on my lips: may the god of thunder and lightning never abandon you, Stutters Grogan.

The rest of my career, everyone knows. It wasn't just boxers who were dancing at fifty beats per minute during those years. Chaplinitis had infected the entire planet, an epidemic. Success had the same time signature as a wild foxtrot.

One of its first consequences was that my brother, Syd, and I could move our mother from Cane Hill to a better asylum, Peckham House, and then later bring her to California. To tell the truth, I worked so much that I rarely managed to visit her, but I was proud to have brought my family together again someplace else. My mother had become calmer with age. For long stretches at a time she seemed simply to be a slightly absent-minded lady, with a yellowed smile and the occasional flicker of the child she once was in her eyes. On her excursions from the asylum, she liked to treat people she came across to ice cream, or else to buy thousands of dollars' worth of silk. I let her. I was happy for her hands to touch everything they had ever desired. A few times I brought her with me on set. But when she saw me emerge from make-up as the Tramp, she told me that I should buy myself a new suit and that I was as pale as a ghost.

'You should spend more time outside, Charlie.'

It was only towards the close of 1925 that I finally got around to the project I had always dreamed of completing, a film about the circus which I've never spoken about much – certainly not in my autobiography – for reasons that will become clear. By now, I was thirty-six years old and on my second marriage, and for some time I had been visited every night by this nightmare: I'm walking on a wire at a dizzying height above the ground. My safety harness comes off and dangles just out of reach. Tugging at my pants is a troupe of crazed monkeys.

So, I began there, with that scene, and whenever I worked on it I immediately fell back into that world of sawdust, laughter, and tears. That's how I put it on the first title card. I guess at heart I remained just that, a title-card writer.

It wasn't an easy film. It took me two years, and there were several interruptions. Everything that could go wrong did go wrong: storms, mistakes, theft. First I lost the big top, then the negatives. One morning a fire destroyed the studios, a disaster that I observed with my own eyes glistening and already made up as the Tramp: broken glass, useless equipment, clouds of ash. My hair went grey overnight. On the last day, our trailers were stolen. I divorced my second wife and a scandal erupted. At this point, even I was tempted to abandon the film.

The truth is that I went ahead only because I knew I had left something half done and because I owed a debt. Of course, I'm also incurably stubborn when it comes to work, and always try to finish what I start. I wanted to recreate for everyone the magic of a travelling circus, just as I had known it as a child. Everything I knew about mime and balance came from the circus, but I still had the sensation of not having finishing my apprenticeship: I still had to learn to walk a tightrope, to ride a bicycle through the air, to communicate with lions.

I worked a great deal on the soundtrack as well. Music has always been part of me. I distinctly recall my mother singing in our room, and a harmonica and a clarinet outside a pub in Kennington Road playing 'The Honeysuckle and the Bee'. How many times did I sing it to you when you were little?

You are my honey, honeysuckle, I am the bee...

In fact, if I hadn't become an actor I would definitely have been a violinist. It is the instrument I love the most, because its voice is closest to a woman's. By then, I had already written melodies for a pair of short films – this was long before I composed music for *The Kid* and a good part of *The Gold Rush*. Thinking about musical accompaniment always helped me find new plot ideas. In the evening after dinner I would take solitary walks and whistle whatever came into my head; when I got back home I would set the notes down on a stave (with a few mistakes, inevitably), and try it again and again for hours on the piano. Of course, to go from that to an arrangement for an entire orchestra was the job of a maestro. His name was Frank and he was a flugelhorn player, the kindest person I ever met. I would hum the motif and then ask him to continue. We understood each other marvellously well, and he must have had telepathic powers, because he always managed to realize what I merely imagined. But that's the way it is, after all – the only telepathy human beings have is called sensibility. Every time maestro Frank called me in for the first play-through, I could hardly contain myself. I would sit alone or with a few others in front of a full orchestra, in an empty United Artists studio, settle back, and listen. Music has always seemed to me like a miracle greater than cinema – no sequence of images has ever moved me as much.

Perhaps it was fitting that it was as a musician that I concluded my career, composing a new score for *The Circus*, a film I'd made half a century earlier. I wrote a song for the film, too – 'Swing Little Girl', which I was even shameless enough to sing myself, at the age of eighty – along with a theme about disappointment in love, and a symphonic finale I'm rather proud of. I am there, in the music. And if you ever feel nostalgic for my voice, seek it out in those sentimental chords, I'm not ashamed of them. There, you'll find every-thing I would have liked to say about life when words were not enough.

That's how it is, you see: in my films the music was actu-ally the story I was trying to tell. In some ways, it always came before the script, because it was my script, guiding my every movement. I knew that everything I shot would be perfectly synchronized with every note because I had already conceived it in terms of dance. If I'd had my way, I would have pro-jected a black square the whole time and left nothing but the heart-rending theme of a tuba. Let the spectators imagine the circus all on their own.

As it was, I opened the film with the sequence of a girl standing up on a white horse as it runs around the ring. It was my homage to Eszter, and to her legendary beauty, which I'd never had the chance to admire in person. During the auditions, I slipped up and called the actress I had chosen for the part by Eszter's name. That evening, I was approached by two of the clowns who get scolded by the impresario in the scene we'd been rehearsing for not being funny.

'Did you know Eszter?' they asked.

Their names were Coluccini and Barrante. When I was casting their roles, I hadn't wanted a pair of actors but rather performers who really came from the circus. These two were already well on in years, but with their white hair and bags under their eyes they seemed perfect for the parts I wanted to give them. One was originally from Italy and had a pointed cap, fat belly, and faded suit; the other was taller and had his forehead, nose, and mouth coloured red, a hat in the shape of a washtub, and a Spanish accent. But it was nature that had given them the melancholy air it would have been impossible to achieve with mere make-up.

'No, I didn't know Eszter, but I heard a great deal about her,' I answered. 'Once I went looking for her, but the only thing I managed to see was the place where she was buried.'

'We worked with her,' said Coluccini, and the reverence in his voice reminded me of the juggler Zarmo's.

'The greatest equestrian acrobat there ever was.'

'We were part of her company.'

'And we continued to be part of it even after she and many others left.'

'We worked all over Britain.'

'At the Hippodrome in London, too.'

I told them that I had also worked at the Hippodrome, towards the end of the last century, as one of Cinderella's cats. They embraced me as if they'd held me at my baptism and never known it.

The fat clown drew a bottle of wine and three glasses from one of his pockets and together we drank to the occasion that had brought us together again and to my brilliant career.

Then to Marceline, who came to a bad end.

To the acrobats who had missed a trick.

To the tamers who had not been obeyed.

To the ballerinas with lips the colour of roses.

To the short-lived dwarves.

To the magicians who needed glasses.

To the black bears.

To the clowns fizzed-out like flat champagne.

To the cross-eyed knife throwers.

To the ones who had taught us our craft.

My two friends had memories like steel traps and went on for some time. For my part, I also lifted my glass for a forgotten actor or two and a few failed screenwriters. When we were completely drunk, the fat clown said something strange.

'This last toast is to Arlequin.'

'Yes, to Arlequin.'

'May he hear us from up on his hill.'

My glass was abruptly forgotten in mid-air, my face incredulous.

'What's up, director?'

'You remember Arlequin, don't you, at the Hippodrome?'

'He was the one who fed the animals…'

I nodded my head slightly.

'He lives in a hospice near London. You didn't know?'

'Plenty of our colleagues are there with him too, all folks who no longer work.'

My head was spinning.

'Arlequin is still alive?'

'Sure, Mr Chaplin.'

I became whiter than chalk.

'I just remembered that I have something to give him,' I said.

As soon as the film was finished and playing in the theatres, I was free to jump on a train and then immediately on a ship.

I hadn't returned to London for many years and each time I did I suffered. Whenever a journalist, with the wistful smile of someone who doesn't know what he's talking about, asks me to recall my childhood, my blood boils. There's nothing evocative or romantic in poverty and hardship, and anyway I've never trusted these kinds of questions. I'm afraid to know what's behind them. The one advantage of my difficult childhood is that I will never become accustomed to luxury. But even when I'm dead, I'll still be accused of egotism, of having been too canny with my financial affairs, of having used the excuse of being kicked out of America by McCarthy as a Bolshevik to flee to Switzerland, with my family, and my money – in short, they won't forgive me for having had all that success and not coming to a bad end. They're galled at the happy ending that Oona, your mother, has given to my life – a happy ending that I, on the contrary, always denied the Tramp.

But having poverty behind me is like having it always ahead of me. I've seen too many lost men and women in those dressing rooms, the face behind the make-up sadder and more discouraged than a sparrow with its wings clipped, hopping along the edge of a deserted balcony until it falls or throws itself in a river: Frank Tinney, Max Linder, Marceline... men who had entertained the world or seduced it, along with countless women whose beauty could not save them, whose names have been erased from history. For me, it's always been a struggle against oblivion. Which is, ultimately, a struggle with Death. And I could hardly forget, tonight of all nights, that he will come to take me in the end. But always, with every new screenplay, every new film... there's not a single one that I didn't shoot with the sensation of risking everything and the awareness that, sooner or later, I would fail. Which is why I've always made hay when the sun was shining. At least on this trip I was seeking out someone who had no need to hear from me on such topics.

This time, I was in London for a week. The first evening I wandered aimlessly along the Thames, then went to eat at a spot in Covent Garden. A man at the next table was reading an American newspaper, the *Los Angeles Times*. I had always enjoyed peeping at other people's newspapers, ever since as a child I used to peek at the images of Sherlock Holmes in *The Strand*. The news seems more interesting when it's stolen.

226

Especially, as it was in this case, if it's from a few days earlier: for me old newspapers have a mysteriously irresistible fascination. That evening, however, I would have done well to keep my eyes on my plate. The man was eating a steak and kidney pie with one hand and holding up the entertainment section in the other. I couldn't help noticing a banner headline. The article was signed by one of the most authoritative critics in California, Slim Anderson. I approached the table and asked if I might borrow the newspaper for a moment. The man reluctantly agreed but continued to stare at me the entire time I took to read the article.

RISE AND FALL OF A CLOWN
CHAPLIN'S STAR PLUNGES INTO THE PACIFIC

In a Santa Monica movie theatre yesterday evening the showing of Charlie Chaplin's latest motion picture, *The Circus*, degenerated into comic turmoil. Believing the director to be present in the hall disguised as a vagrant, the public became so enraged as to surround the unlucky man and bombard him with insults until finally recognizing their mistake.

As of yesterday we may remove the name Charlie Chaplin from the list of movie stars and add it to that of the most splendid comets to have crossed the Los Angeles sky and landed shamefully in the sea. The public's violent and unambiguous reaction brings to an end, for good one hopes, the career of this horrible clown. To sum up his new feature, *The Circus*, one need only turn to a series of adjectives: shameless, insolent, provocative, vexing, incoherent, illogical, disjointed, unpleasant, boring... but there's one that can stand in for them all: ridiculous. *The Circus* offends every rule of storytelling and is as much a crime against common sense as against aesthetics.

Nonetheless, to the many ingenuous defects of this demented picture, let us add the one that in all likelihood did most trouble spectators' souls, namely the morbid insistence on humanity's most unseemly and disgusting details. For a full hour every form of human deformity filed past, without regard for any sense of decency, before our incredulous, horrified eyes. Pathetic jokes of nature, freaks and aberrations and other implausible monsters filled every corner of the screen: sad, fingerless clowns, walking skeletons, backwards men, sadistic impresarios and fathers, thieves... The few children in the audience began to cry while their mothers tried in vain to cover their eyes. It was by now abundantly clear that an already fragile, coarse, and shaky plot was nothing but a pretext for displaying the wretched imperfection of the world. And for belittling, as Chaplin has always done, every constituted authority, from policemen to the army. What, moreover, can we expect from someone who, still in the bloom of his youth, ran away from the war? Fortunately, the theatre owner, in the face of the audience's rage, decided to suspend the humiliating spectacle. The event confirms just how much the cinema, more than any other profession, is today exposed to the enormous proliferation of impostors, scoundrels, and cheats who have gained undeserved fame. It falls to our critical gaze as American citizens and public witnesses to prevent the perversion of its function. The Santa Monica episode is a clear warning to those who wish to colonize our consciousness and blind us with their charlatanism.

Before the man's startled eyes I tore out the page from his newspaper, put it in my pocket, and hurried out of the establishment. For years afterwards, I continued to read this article in secret, as one reads something clandestine shut up in one's room, afraid that someone might burst in at any moment. It was the only significant negative review *The Circus* received, but there was something in it that I needed to focus on, something that I had been hiding from myself. Ever since my boxing days, I've been someone who is able to take a lot of punishment. I charged a dollar per round, five cents per blow, give or take. A reasonable wage, for sure. But never ever before, no matter how many insults and punches rained down on me, had my lips trembled or my eyes watered as they did when I read that article. The charge of having depicted 'the wretched imperfection of the world' still strikes me as undeserved praise, but this only consoled me a little. On other occasions I had always given as good as I got, if not better. And yet, if that evening Slim Anderson himself had appeared before me, I wouldn't have known what to say. His words had hit the mark. Not the skewer of adjectives he had roasted for me. Or the old slander of having evaded military service. I continued to receive insults and white feathers in the mail, but it also occasionally happened that valiant soldiers would send me their own medals, in thanks for having entertained them in the improvised theatres at the front. No, that wasn't it with Anderson, the matter went much deeper. It was the accusation of fraud that hurt the most. I didn't care to sink my paws into the mire of self-pity – I could have drowned there, ever since the days when I was so hungry I'd pick up apples from below the tables of London markets – but I had suspected from the beginning that the cinema would only prove a phase in my life. There was no point in kidding myself: I would always be a fish out of water in that environment, just as I was in America. And yet I had let myself be dragged along by the current all the same. A fleet of butterflies had taken up residence in my head, every pair of wings displaying a rainbow of lies. It was my ingenuousness that made me angry. Slim Anderson was right: I was nothing more than a hastily improvised autodidact, a neighbourhood pickpocket, a braggart. Better to get out now, and quietly, before some Attorney General, wielding a decree of the Republic, denied me a re-entry visa to the United States, or a residency permit. To close up shop, clear out, pull up stakes – say it how you like: I would have done better to hang up my movie camera.

Indeed, this wasn't a great moment for me. I was tired and depressed. I had thought *The Circus* would be my crowning achievement; instead I feared it would be the last work I ever did. I even considered moving to China. But in the end, I knew I had to get on with completing my secret mission, as I referred to it with my friends without being taken seriously. I would deliver what I had held on to for almost twenty years to its rightful owner, and then, as soon as I returned to California, I would withdraw all copies of that film from circulation and find myself a new profession.

Rose Park.

A fragrant name for a hospice, I thought.

I had asked around in London: people had heard of a place of that name on the outskirts, but they thought it was a private hospital. For the mentally unbalanced, old schizophrenics and hypochondriacs who no longer had anyone left in this world to look after them. 'If you want to rejuvenate your brain, friend, that's the right place,' said a man with a pint of beer in the doorway of a pub. 'They give you a nice little shock, and poof! You're set. Even a tiny mistake, though, and you come back down the hill more feeble-minded than my granny. You're better off with beer for such things. Think about it, there's still time to change your mind. First one's on me, if you like.'

I thanked him, but said that I had an appointment.

He turned his back on me, offended.

When I arrived at the front gate, the first thing I saw were women in white coats crossing the garden. They floated past like visions. But I only had to cross the threshold to realize what kind of place this was. Rose Park was nothing but a refuge for clowns gone sad, acrobats with rusty bones, brittle as sand, solitary illusionists who had never caught a break, jugglers whose hands trembled, female performers who'd let themselves go, and ruined impresarios who never stopped talking. These were people hardened by misfortune and neglect, merely waiting for pneumonia or a heart attack to take them away once and for all, one after the other. It was a gigantic waiting room.

But there's nothing more stubbornly resistant to death

than a circus or theatre man. Coluccini said as much, repeatedly and with evident satisfaction, as we finished the film. His aim was to reach 120 years, out of mere spite against oblivion and the ingratitude of men. Barrante, the Spanish clown, had the same goal. I called them the 120 Club.

On one side of the garden, a small crowd of men and women sat chatting. I approached. It sounded like they were talking about old tours. Who knows how many times they had already told each other these stories, but there can't have been much else left for them to do. When they became aware of me they fell silent and stared at me as though sizing up a new arrival. I was still young, but I might have had a major reversal of fortune or nervous breakdown, you never know at what age a career might finish.

'Are you looking for someone?' a fellow as tall as a street lamp asked me.

'I'm looking for Arlequin,' I replied. 'I was told he lived here.'

'He's upstairs, in his room,' said a woman with a heavily made-up mouth.

I bowed to her and headed towards the building at the centre of the park, a small villa from another time. Before reaching the door I noticed that along the edge of the gravel path, under the trees, three or four wooden easels with pencil drawings had been left out. I stopped to look. The corners of the sheets of paper flapped in the wind. The first drawing was of a rearing horse, but abandoned in mid-air, with its front hooves flailing and nothing below, as if whoever had sketched it had suddenly broken off with a nervous gesture and flung the pencil away. No, I reflected then, normally an artist would have sketched out the complete figure before filling in details; these were wilfully different. The other drawings were also incomplete: animals and men of which only a part could be seen, the rest merely guessed at. A catalogue of interrupted actions: hobbled steps, mutilated looks, split lips just beginning to break the silence.

'These were drawn by the man you're looking for,' said a young, white-coated woman whom I hadn't heard approach.

'Arlequin?'

'Everyone here thinks he's a bit touched, but they let him draw and talk to himself. Are you a relative?'

'No,' I said with difficulty. 'I worked with him once, but I was just a child.'

'He'll be pleased to see you, but don't stay too long.'

'Okay.'

'And try not to get upset.'

'I've seen other people in his condition.'

'Sometimes he clenches his fists, as if his hands ached, then he throws himself on the bed and starts shaking.'

'Is that why he doesn't finish the drawings?'

'I don't know. I like to think that it's his personal protest against all the things that are perfect, and then go wrong. That's why he draws horses with only two hooves, men with just one eye, soldiers missing an arm...'

'Maybe he's right, maybe it would've been better if we'd all come into the world crippled from the beginning.'

'Maybe.'

'Learning to part with perfection is too painful, and pursuing it all one's life is a proud and useless gesture.'

'Sounds like a line from Shakespeare.'

'I don't remember any more who said it.'

'You're Charlie Chaplin, aren't you?'

'Yes…'

'I recognized you right away, though no one else here would have. Dressed like this, you seem like such a normal person.'

'I am a normal person. Incomplete, like Arlequin's drawings.'

The woman smiled.

'You should see your friend. When he stands there, with his pencil, then everyone within the walls of this garden stops, and a kind of miracle happens, like it does when people watch your films, and the broken lines of the horse seem complete to them.'

'Would that I were capable of such magic.'

'Your character is.'

'What do you mean?'

'As I see it, the Tramp is a whiteface clown, with his air of sad, ruined nobility, and at the same time he's an Auguste clown, the irreverent buffoon, the naughty child who pulls faces and whose hands are always dirty – he combines the two souls of every clown. It seems to me that, until you came along, no one in the whole history of the circus had ever managed that.'

I was touched.

'That's one of the nicest things anyone has ever said about the Tramp.'

'Well, it's true.

'And you? Have you worked here long?'

'Long enough. But you've come all the way up here for a

reason, I imagine, and I don't want to take up any more of your time. Go up to the first floor. If you find someone there, tell them you spoke with Elisabeth.'

'I will. Thank you, Elisabeth, it's been a pleasure to speak with you.'

'For me too.'

I glanced again at the drawing of the house on the piece of paper nearest us, with its unplastered rock wall, incomplete roof, and half-open window. I imagined Arlequin standing before the picture, the others crowded around.

'He drew it again and again, every day,' Elisabeth said now. 'If he was having a good day, he'd also draw himself behind the house. Or half of himself, that is.'

'Who taught him how to draw like this?'

'A Spaniard in the circus, he told us.'

I gave Elisabeth's name at the entrance and they let me pass. The walls in the stairway had been scraped almost bare. They must have been green, once, dark green below and a lighter shade above, but now only a few patches of paint could be made out, mostly clustered around the line of transition. A series of rooms opened onto the first-floor corridor. There were no doors, so it was possible to see inside. It seemed indecent, but I didn't avert my eyes. In cell after cell I saw old men seated on the edge of a bed, or standing on the same tile square, endlessly repeating the same movement. Some swayed, as if rocking themselves to sleep on an invisible trapeze, others spoke aloud as they gazed into the white plaster vault.

I recalled my mother one evening in our garret, kissing

bread, tearing it, pressing small bits of it to her chest and head, as if it were ashes in an Easter rite, then furiously stashing pieces away, the gesture of an animal trying to hoard food.

I took a few more steps.

His was the second to last room.

He had his back towards me.

He had become gaunt in his old age, but his figure retained its dignity, despite being irreparably hunched forward. With a table before him, he looked like a cobbler bent over his workbench. Next I noticed the scraggly white beard. I stared at his profile, his cracked lips, straight nose, deeply furrowed forehead, wispy grey hair, and deep-set black eyes. But most of all I was struck by his hands. They continued in their task, not at all put off by my presence, sure of what they were doing. I shifted my gaze to the paper on which he drew. Nothing but a labyrinth of senseless lines, a tangle of knotted string, a spider's web rolled up into a ball by the fingers of a giant.

It is only when I open the suitcase I have with me that Arlequin turns in my direction.

'This belongs to you,' I say.

Arlequin is agitated. He must have heard me coming up the stairs, but he knows that it's not a visiting day. And yet no one else, surely, has come to visit him in twenty years. Maybe just a dwarf, once, who knows. He has nevertheless weighed my every step down the corridor, understood that I was heading in his direction, towards his room. He sensed me enter. Maybe he thinks I'm curious about his drawing, which I now see is a kind of giant fruit, inside which he has written words that no one will understand, one on top of another.

He delicately takes the letter I hold out to him and reads his name on the envelope. I hear his breath come up short. Before I become paralysed by emotion I reach again into my suitcase and pull out his wooden box. I move Arlequin's incomprehensible drawing from the table and set the box down there. Arlequin watches me carefully, but with the bewildered air of someone who no longer knows what is about to happen.

You invented it just in time, I want to tell him.

Instead it is Arlequin's mouth that moves, but he doesn't speak immediately.

He extends a hand and clasps mine. He's trembling; it must be years since he last shook another man's hand. Then, as he no longer has the teeth he needs to hold back the words:

'So much time has passed.'

And his face lights up like an old oil lamp.

He takes the box and leaves the room with shuffling steps, continues down the length of the corridor, descends the bare-walled stairway. I go to the window and watch him move, with a slowness not born of caution, across the lawn. Eventually, he reaches the farthest bench in the park, takes a seat, steadies the box on his lap, and finally he lowers his eyes...

I know what he's seeing.

The sandy circus ring,
    clubs, bolas, and hoops in mid-air,
    men in livery filing out of the ring,

a troupe of clowns,

the pitch-dark that conceals an audience,

the entrance together of six horses at a trot,

some clad in sparkling harness: jumping saddles, martingales, breastplates, stirrups; others with only mouthpieces and reins that fall on shiny coats,

each has a differently shaped mark on its head: a diamond between the ears or a flower above the nose or a long white stripe from forehead to muzzle,

they circle the ring flank to flank, tossing their manes and tails as if vainly conscious of their own beauty,

they fall in at the centre of the ring according to a precise pattern, bringing their heads together in the form of a star, then trotting backwards and opening up the shape, finally walking their hindquarters around forty-five degrees, a spellbinding spiral,

when the figure is complete, from beneath the belly of one of them springs forth a ballerina, in a bright costume and with a whip in her hand,

she seems to have been born in that moment, from the stomach of the horse,

an apparition to make your heart stop,

in a sudden spin she lifts herself up into the saddle of the animal and cracks the whip above her head,

the herd seems to go wild, rising up on their hind legs and neighing fiercely,

a second crack of the whip shatters the spiral design,

the ring is transformed into a stampede of unruly, rebellious beasts running from side to side, swerving around each other, changing direction,

Eszter dances above them,

her agility is outrageous,

she jumps from one horse to another, at speed, always falling back into the saddle after dizzying somersaults in mid-air, as if she knew the animals' movements in advance,

Arlequin's eyes are fixed on Eszter, not losing sight of her for a moment;

his fingers open and close their grip,

from group routines, Eszter moves on to duets with individual horses, and these are irresistible waltzing turns, the entire repertoire of a mad tightrope walker,

the final flip is so high that for a few seconds Eszter leaves the frame,

Arlequin watches her come back down, but only to disappear again into the fray of muscles and hooves,

the horses diligently regain their original shape, six all in a row, take up the trot again, and exit the ring,

one's first impression is that the horses have crushed her, that her lifeless, disfigured body will now appear trampled into the ground,

but hoof prints are all that is left behind.

If that scene had been projected onto a wall, at this point one would hear the sound of a strip of film becoming detached from the reel and beginning to slap against the wheel of the projector, the wingbeats of a bird thrashing with desperate insistency against a window, but that scene is contained within a crank-operated box and does not make any noise.

Arlequin stands and takes a few unsteady steps towards the centre of the garden.

I approach his latest drawing and all the sentences written there are suddenly clear.

Now I remember…

I have no right to stay there. I stand up too. I walk back down the length of the corridor, race down the stairs, and return to the garden.

Once she caressed my face. I had fallen asleep on a chest, and no one else was around. She touched my cheek. I pretended to be still sleeping.

Arlequin is sitting on the grass.

He has the letter from Eszter, open, in his hands.

A crowd of ghosts gathers before me: Zarmo and Marceline, Yitzhak Gabor, Makrouhi, Viola, her mulatto daughter Naima…

I touch his shoulder and walk away.

I didn't know that remembering was like being seized by cramp.

From a distance, I see him closing one hand over the other, and it seems to me I see him sink his fingernails into the skin.

I can still feel the heat from the tip of her finger.

I promise myself that I will leave for Los Angeles as soon as possible, to start all over again.

A cool breeze strikes me in the face.

At the centre of the garden a horse rears up and an acrobat bends over backwards, holding tight to the reins, until her long blonde hair touches the sandy ground, as her costume shimmers under the lights of the circus, and everything there finally appears to me returned, for all time, to the frail imperfection of equilibrium.

Behind me Arlequin moves through the park, a firefly blithely flitting through a holly wood.

All of this, dear Christopher, took place long, long before I met your mother. She doesn't know most of it, but I want to confess it all to you now. Time is running out.

As soon as I returned to Hollywood I gave the order for my film to be withdrawn from theatres. The next morning I hastily tossed some things into a suitcase and hung my long overcoat with the astrakhan collar back in the closet. The clothes I wore the day I arrived in America still fitted me perfectly. I had kept them all that time and in putting them on I realized how worn they already were back then. There was no need for me to put make-up on. I left the moustache in its box and didn't bother to dye my hair. Nobody would have recognized me. I had gone back to being an anonymous forty-year-old vagabond on the road in America, like so many others in those years, with their hand-me-down clothes and a wool blanket across their shoulders.

I don't know if my feet had already decided which direction they would take, but the following day I found myself in the San Francisco train station. A railwayman's waving flag announced the imminent departure of a train bound for Sacramento. I bought the ticket and climbed aboard. They closed the door right behind me. The train lurched and anyone still standing up was nearly sent tumbling; it moved forwards a bit, backwards a bit, as if shaking off all its rust.

Then.

Then slowly the iron wheels began to turn.

One following the other.

Tuntùn tuntùn.

Tuntùn tuntùn.

They hadn't completed three revolutions before I knew my destination.

In Sacramento I would buy another ticket for the First Transcontinental Railroad.

Tuntùn tuntùn.

As far as Omaha.

Tuntùn tuntùn.

And from there to Youngstown.

Tuntùn tuntùn, tuntùn tuntùn, tuntùn tuntùn.

By now the train was flying through open country covered with frost.

Youngstown. Suddenly I felt Naima's hands tending to my bruises all those years ago and I cursed myself in every language I knew for my obtuseness. If I had an appointment with anyone, anywhere in the world, it was with her. I felt like I always did before shooting the key scene in a film, with the same electricity coursing through my body at the mere foretaste of it, that scene... In my agitation I began to laugh uncontrollably. A gentleman got up and moved quickly away, afraid of having to travel next to a madman who laughed like Chaplin.

Youngstown greeted me a week later with its usual show of unconcern. The houses were the same colour as before, some white, some rusty; the trolley still rattled down the centre of the high street, while many more automobiles lined its pavements; and the welcome sign still swayed in the wind, though the wood was split, the paint peeling, like a slogan gone out of fashion.

I don't know what I expected, but everything was going about its own business, evidently indifferent to my return. Only the bench where I had sat down once before had the air of a widow, patiently waiting for me in the tree-lined square. I collapsed onto the seat. It was with a certain satisfaction that I observed the Dollar Bank building: the enormous letters of its sign at the top no longer mocked me. My pockets were full of dollars now. And yet I wasn't happy.

It took everything I had to travel the distance between that bench and Viola and Eszter's flower shop. My legs felt heavier than lead, like the character in a fairy tale that my mother always used to read me, who could only be saved by a creature lighter than a feather.

As I turned onto South Avenue I was nearly overcome by fatigue. I stopped across the street from the shop.

Naima was on her feet inside.

I could see her through the window.

She was speaking to a customer, a tall woman with a long face who gave the impression of being in a hurry. Naima showed her various flowers, advised her on what to choose. She lifted up a bunch of gardenias and only then did I realize the delicacy of which she was capable in every gesture. She treated everything with respect, as if everything demanded it, as though she was returning elegance and dignity to the world with her understated care. How had I failed to see it before? She was all that remained of Eszter. The acrobat must have taught her all her secrets, as she would have a daughter. All her equilibrist's tricks, the mystery of her lightness. I was absolutely sure that if she'd wanted to, Naima would have been capable of performing a breathtaking series of backflips

243

on that very pavement in front of the shop. Her hair was pulled back in a ponytail falling to her shoulders and the flash of her smile lit up her face with every expression.

She turned her eyes towards me, a gaze that penetrated my every fibre, pushing into my dishevelled hair, my short, nervous legs, the folds of my threadbare jacket, and I suddenly felt sorry for myself, for how I must have looked to her, for what I was and for what I would be. For my unhappiness, despite worldwide success. I hoped for her not to remember me. But then, terrified, I saw her calmly lay aside the gardenias, politely take her leave of the tall woman, exit the shop, and walk towards me. She approached slowly, took my hand and held it between hers for a long time.

'… You?'

There was no need for us to say anything else that morning.

When I followed her home that night and she turned the key in the lock, I was astonished to find no one inside. 'You have to promise me something, Charlie,' Naima said. 'As long as you're here, you won't ask me any questions.'

'As you wish.'

'It's a deal then?'

'It's a deal.'

Naima led me down the hallway, across the sitting room where I had been received the first time, to the little bedroom that had been mine for nearly a month. I made out the bed and the wardrobe, and the window behind the curtains. Naima turned to me and caressed my face. I think it was the first real caress I had received from a woman for a long time. It felt different from the touch of all the other women I had met in those years. All at once, something cold and hard in me melted. I remained standing there, dazed by the darkness and by the warmth of her hand in the midst of all that silence.

'Do you remember what bad shape you were in when they brought you here that day?'

'To tell the truth, I don't remember much.'

'Who would have believed it then: the least known actor in the world... You were all swollen, your face was as big as a pumpkin, two black eyes, your hair matted and dirty, but even like that you made me laugh.'

'Not even bruises take me seriously...'

'You're lucky. But now, Charlie, go to bed, I'm sure you're tired. The sheets on the bed are clean.'

'Thank you, good night.'

'Good night to you too, Charlie.'

When I woke the following day the sun was already high in the sky. Naima was in the kitchen making breakfast.

'You have to open the shop,' I said to her.

'No, not today.'

The light from the window above the sink fell diagonally across her pale brown skin. Naima took a tin of biscuits from a cupboard. She moved through space with the naturally firm step of someone devoting her complete attention to what she is doing, and this rendered her so beautiful, free, vulnerable. She poured some milk for me, and a little later we went out.

Soon the rows of houses on the outskirts of Youngstown dwindled and the countryside took over. It must have recently rained for a long time; the terrain had turned into a muddy, puddle-strewn plain. And yet, for all that the wet weather had

245

transformed it, the landscape did not feel alien to me. I began to recognize it as we followed the long curve of the path and came alongside a wooden fence. We were climbing a hillside of maples and holly and our destination was clear to me even before I saw the rows of headstones cropping up in the middle of the swamp.

We entered the cemetery, dragging our feet through the mire. Oak Hill was deserted that morning, and the only sound that spread over the endless expanse was the noise of our shoes, passing birds, leaves shaking in the wind. We made our way past an array of inscribed headstones; the infill paint on some had faded, and the names could only be read by tracing a finger along the grooves in the stones. Some dates had disappeared, others survived, in a jumble of numbers that restored to my eyes all the paradoxical unreality of life.

Shortly before reaching the cobbler Andy Vargas and the attorney Hubert Moore whom I remembered being buried beside Eszter, Naima stopped in front of two stones that must have been planted there within the past few years. She walked up to the first one, sat back on her heels, and dug her hands into the mud. It didn't take her long to find what she was looking for. From the muck she extracted a wooden walking stick, long and knotty, wiped the earth away, and leaned it against the headstone.

I stepped forward. I read the name of Makrouhi Dolmayan, born Hrazdan, 1831; died Youngstown, 1916.

Then that of Viola Baldwin: Chicago, 1848 – Yo-Town, 1917. The headstone belonging to Eszter Neumann stood a few yards away.

'At sunset, on sunny days, the shade of that oak embraces

all three of them,' said Naima. 'The man who looks after this place was very kind and allowed me to bury them near each other.'

'How did it happen?'

'They slipped away, one after the other, in the space of a few months, overcome by a silent illness with no symptoms. I watched them melt away, day after day, burning down like a pair of candles. They died in the same way: first they lost their words, then all the heat in their bodies. From their feet, their legs, their hands. Only the skin around the heart remained warm still, and their eyes wide open, to capture what little they still could of the light. My mother's eyes too, even though they were blind. In the end, their breath was all that was left. For hours. A loud whistling, like a protest, then just weak puffs of air. Until they sank into inexistence. Like walking out into the water farther and farther, and eventually going under. My mother had one last contraction and stretched out her fingers in farewell.'

I lowered my eyes out of respect.

'It's incomprehensible to me that we could suddenly stop being together, stop talking, stop touching, and that this absence will last for ever. At home, almost every day, I find myself talking to an empty chair.'

'I'm sorry, Naima. I had a lot to ask both of them, I only realize it now.'

'My mother said that whatever question you might have asked her, I was your answer, and that one day you would discover that.'

'Come with me to California, Naima. I'll make you a movie star...'

247

'What is this, Mr Chaplin, a job offer?'

I couldn't have separated the laughter from the tears in her voice.

'You are the answer, now.'

'It's a real shame we've come to this so late,' she said. 'It's like it always is in your movies: at the end the Tramp heads off alone down a country road like this one, swaying his shoulders.'

I tried to raise a hand, but Naima placed a finger over my lips. Then she started off back home.

That night, for the last time, I went to sleep in the bed where I had convalesced. The Youngstown night weighed on me like London's had when I lived in a garret. In a few hours' time, I would be on board a train that would redeliver me definitively to the splendours and spite of Hollywood, to all the films I would still make and to those I never would. I turned towards the wall, my eyes closed, thinking of the bright lights of Los Angeles, and of the dark periods of exile I would inevitably have to undergo. I didn't open my eyes, even when Naima lay down beside me. I could almost feel the perfect arc of her body, but I preferred to imagine it solely on the basis of the irregular curves of her breath. Naima remained like that for a bit, without touching me, while I continued to pretend to sleep. Then she got up and left the room. Finally I fell asleep. The following morning I awoke before dawn. I went out into the hallway and stopped in front of the door to her room. It was open, her hips gently swelled the bed-sheets. I knew that she was awake as I had been, just hours earlier, but all the same I tried to move quietly. I lay down beside her for a few minutes, without touching her, merely stealing a bit of the warmth that her body transmitted across the inches between us. As dawn broke and the world around us returned to life, I rose with a strength I didn't think I possessed. I left behind those sheets, that house, that landscape of hills and factories that re-emerged through the windows and that could have been mine and hers. I closed my suitcase, dressed, and made my way to the train station.

Desire. That's the theme of life and it was the theme of Calvero, the last clown I played. And, of course, my Monsieur Verdoux thought so, too. He was one of the most controversial masks I ever stole from real life, in this case from the news. He was a fellow with the habit of marrying old ladies and then burning them in his kitchen oven, taking the homicidal logic of capitalism to its extreme consequences. But it's a form of desire, all the same. Simply put, life cannot exist without desire. They'll tell you that sexual trauma is what shapes your personality. Pay them no heed – the real trauma is poverty, whereas only the bourgeois consider sex to be a disease. When I was young, I promised myself I would have a girlfriend for every letter of the alphabet: Agnes, Barbara, Carole, Dorothy… Love would be my dictionary. From that moment on I've never met a woman without asking myself if I would like to kiss her or not. It's a question I still ask myself, if you'll pardon my saying so, but it doesn't mean I love your mother any less.

And yet, for some time now I've often found myself thinking that desire is also what's behind all of human stupidity, vulgarity, cruelty, and infantilism. Desire has made me ridiculous so many times, not just in the eyes of the world but to myself as well. It's made me insensitive, and an idiot, and put me in danger. As a poet once wrote, I've arrived at the point of desiring not to desire anything any more. I would like to warn you against it, but that would be pointless. Hypocrisy makes us not want to talk about it, but it's the most powerful force out there and no one is immune, not at any age. Your fifteen years are as good as all of mine; I may have the benefit of experience, but I'm every bit as vulnerable as you. You're still a boy, Christopher, and you will fall in love many times, and you too will have to create for yourself the kind of imperfection that humans crave, that never actually exists in nature, the imperfection of some equilibrium. I say imperfection because every equilibrium is imperfect. Life, by its very nature, cannot remain in equilibrium: it's too crooked and unstable for that. And yet, we humans stil crave it. So, all my exuberance, all this desire, along with all my desperate shyness, in the end I poured them all into the cinema, and the cinema saved me. Because everything vanishes, but not the desires we have.

Yes, the cinema saved me and has gone on saving me, though a lifetime has passed since I made my last film. The only difference is that now, instead of trying to win over a studio boss or an audience, I've been trying to win over the ultimate critic: Death himself. The first time I cheated him was the most difficult. I reproduced all of my old gags and tricks, but he remained cold and impassive. I felt again the panic that had gripped me the first time I went onstage in New York, together with Stan Laurel, when the New World baptized us with a fiasco. I was close to tears: not because I'd failed to raise a laugh, but because I didn't want to die without seeing you grow up. And in the end, it was only the utter helplessness of my old age that did the trick. When he saw my decrepitude, Death began to laugh. Like Mack Sennett in the Keystone Studios, like anyone else who saw me at work in the glory years. And because he was amused by my infirmity, he granted me another year's grace and then disappeared. It took several hot water bottles and some mugo pine salve for me to recuperate from my back pain, but I was still alive.

From then on I took advantage of every pretext offered to me by old age: weakening sight, memory loss, regrets for the passing of youth. My own condition offered me an inexhaustible repertoire. The trick, though, remains the same as it always has been: to bungle something and in so doing turn the world upside down and backwards. The comedic mechanism is a subversive one. If a giant tries every which way to open a door and doesn't succeed, but right away the door opens effortlessly for a cat, a child, a poor tramp or an old man, we laugh. Because it's the complete opposite of what happens in life. Comedy is a somersault, a man who gets up after taking a tumble, a man who is always on the point of falling but never does. Comedy is a lefty like me. It mocks the rich, restores hope, redresses injustice. As Frank Capra used to say, it closes the door in the face of bullies and opens it to the weak and defenceless, even if only for the flash of a smile. And it's our incredulity at our overturned expectations that makes us laugh until we cry. From the very beginning, when I sang the Jack Jones song in my mother's place, provoking laughter and tears was my infantile protest against poverty, illness, and contempt, and my rejection of hate and of all the destructive habits that never cease to shape human relations. It's amazing, when you think about how highly contagious cheerfulness is, that the world remains so sad and sick.

Every Christmas until this one, I've managed to wring at least a chuckle out of Death and save myself. But tonight, Christopher, I will fail. Tonight of all nights, when I feel so terribly good, my head clear and my legs sturdy as they haven't been for years, and I feel sure I'll be capable of a perfect gag, at the first take, in a way that I never pulled off, even in my best films. There's still no one who can play the drunk better than I can. Tonight, I'll smoke a match in place of the cigarette for the last time. It will be my swan song, the final illusion. But he won't laugh, I can feel it. People do not love perfection, and beyond this I cannot improve.

Tomorrow they will bring you into my room, and you will see me laid out on the bed. When they took me to see my father, at St Thomas's Hospital, I ran away, but I was younger than you are, and the man who lay before me was a stranger. My compassion for him came later, when I too feared losing everything. With my mother, on the other hand, I nearly led her by the hand. She had been hospitalized for an infection, just a few months after the premiere of *The Circus*. On the last day I heard her compliment a nurse on the necklace of glass and wooden beads she had at her neck. I promised her she would get better and I made her laugh for hours. But that night she sat up in bed and said: 'Help me, Charlie.' On the death certificate, I wrote that she had been born a year later than she had, so that her vanity would be flattered in the afterlife as well.

I know, I'm growing sentimental. *Mala música*, my friend Picasso would have said. But it's my music, and I can no longer change it. In my entire life I haven't written more than a dozen letters, but I had time for this one, and that's enough for me. And now, the familiar hooded figure has just arrived. He's right here, in the armchair beneath the window, waiting for me. He knows I haven't left this villa for two months, not since the night in October when I took you to see the unmistakable big top of the Circus Knie.

In a little while you will all come to call me for dinner, you and your mother, your brothers and sisters, your nieces and nephews, but I will already be out strolling with Death, on the obscene moon, who knows where. But don't worry about me, I'm not afraid. My whole life, I've always felt on the verge of a move somewhere new.

We've reached the closing credits, dear Christopher, and I can only be grateful for your acrobatic patience if you have held out so long in the face of all this chatter. For once, I have not been faithful to my principle that every story should be like a tree that you shake and everything you don't need falls to the ground, leaving only the essential. This letter is not a film, and I wanted you to know everything, because I no longer recall where it is that I hid the truth. It would be wonderful to disappear with one last abracadabra. On an airship, a train, or a hot-air balloon. But, all in all, I'm happy enough to ride off astride nothing but my words.

They say that the universe was born from a great, incomprehensible explosion. If you ask me, it must have happened in a circus ring. A woman was vaulting through the air and a man captured it in a magic box, and he reproduced it again and again and again, until he populated the earth, and filled it with sawdust, with laughter, with tears. It could not have happened any other way, I think, because it is only in the disorder of love that any acrobatic feat is possible.

Bye

Your father, Charles

Interior, Night.
24 December 1977

Death sits in Charlie's armchair.

The Tramp lays his pencil down on the desk, and stands. He has the hiccups. He touches his throat. Takes a step, but doesn't manage to stay upright. Knocks into something, a pen holder, makes the catch. Smiles, happy with his reflexes, but then he sets it down in mid-air. The pen holder falls to the ground and all its contents spill out across the floor. The Tramp beholds the disaster, upset, then shrugs his shoulders. Takes another step and slips on a fountain pen. The drunkard. He gets back up, smarting, tries to remove a glove from an already gloveless hand. Finds a cigarette in his pocket, looks at it, then tries in vain to light a match. When finally he succeeds, he brings it to his mouth in place of the cigarette...

DEATH: Enough, Tramp – enough, Charlie.

CHARLIE: If we were in a theatre, even the seats would be laughing.

DEATH: But we're not in a theatre.

CHARLIE: I could go on all night.

DEATH: I know.

CHARLIE: (*slurring his words*) I've never been so drunk.

DEATH: You said yourself that perfection is cruel. You
            didn't make a single mistake, Charlie.

CHARLIE: Really?

DEATH: Yes, but you didn't make me laugh this time.

CHARLIE: I imagine it would also be pointless if I were
            to pretend to enter a lion's cage, or to walk a
            tightrope while a troupe of monkeys try to
            pull me down.

DEATH: Pointless indeed.

CHARLIE: How about the act with the Tramp as
            millionaire, the first one I ever created?

The Tramp swings his cane and hits himself in the leg.

DEATH: Pointless as well.

CHARLIE: I expected as much.

DEATH: In the end you lived six more years than you
            had coming to you.

The Tramp sighs.

CHARLIE: It was a fair deal.

DEATH: But now you must come with me: eighty-eight is
            a fine number to go out on. No matter which
            way you look at it, the value doesn't change. For
            the Chinese it's the sign of double happiness,
            for others it's a symbol of the universe.

CHARLIE: You're right, it's a good number. I'm sorry to

have kept you waiting. For a long time I wanted
to step out with the Tramp again, to have the
little fellow appear in one more film.

DEATH: Why didn't you?

CHARLIE: There was no place for him any more in this
world. But in the end, I got to play him for you.
You've seen his final performances, and you've
laughed a lot. It's a shame about tonight, of
course, but as last audiences go, I can consider
myself satisfied.

*Death falls silent. He absent-mindedly brushes his hands. The
gesture looks familiar, and Charlie pauses for a moment, trying
to place it.*

DEATH: Are you afraid?

CHARLIE: No, I've died so many times onstage.

DEATH: Let's go, some fresh air will do you good.

*Charlie and Death walk out to the terrace, and set forth into the
starry night sky. But then the great actor stops, as if once more in
the limelight, a perfectly weighted pause.*
   He smiles.

CHARLIE: Have you ever seen such a beautiful moon?

Death stares silently at him. Charlie studies him calmly.
   *The full moon becomes a sickle, and from a sickle returns to
being a full moon.*

CHARLIE: Will you permit me one last question?

DEATH: Go on.

CHARLIE: Arlequin, old chap, why did you invent the cinema?

Both suspended in mid-air, as one by one the stars begin to go out, like the lights in a theatre, Death and Charlie look at each other.

DEATH: You've guessed, then?

An ashen light illuminates Charlie's face; he squints.

DEATH: I wanted to learn what it felt like when you knew you would never see a loved one, or the love of your life, ever again.

CHARLIE: Now you know?

DEATH: I never wanted this day to come.

CHARLIE: And that's why you always let me win our little wager?

DEATH: No, we had fun together. And now, taking you away with me is such sorrow…

Charlie grimaces.
Death bows his head.

CHARLIE: It's not your fault, Arlequin, we both knew it would happen.

DEATH: I invented the cinema for Eszter. So that some trace of her splendour would endure. And for you. People will be laughing at you for ever.

I wanted to give mortals this immortal theatre of ceaselessly flickering shadows, to offer them some little compensation for what I was taking from them.

CHARLIE: I know.

Arlequin lets out a barely perceptible sigh. He pulls back his hood; his fingers are dirty with earth. Charlie takes him by the arm.

CHARLIE: Arlequin, old chap, there's no film without a beginning and an end, and this is a good ending. Let's go, before the moon disappears as well.

The pair set off, seen from behind, singing Tu le tu le tu le wa and other old music-hall favourites...

CLOSING CREDITS

I was a boy when I first read Chaplin's autobiography, and have returned to it ever since. As the French writer Jean-Claude Izzo had it: the adventure that you have read is entirely imaginary, even if there are many real events in it.

But I must confess to having also borrowed some names from other stories. The boxer Stutters Grogan, for example, can be found, older and further along in his career, in Paul Auster's *Mr Vertigo*. I glimpsed the glowing, star-strewn ceiling of the Bastiani travelling circus at the end of W.G. Sebald's *Austerlitz*. And you can find Coluccini, the old clown originally from Italy, travelling through Argentina, in the pages of *Shadows* by Osvaldo Soriano, even if he does claim to be a retired acrobat. I admit to owing a lot to the many interviews Chaplin gave, and to David Robinson, his principal biographer. I have indebted myself to the tune of at least a pair of metaphors to Gianni Mura, and I owe a bandolier of ideas to Massimo Paradiso (who I'm positive Mr Fritz would have hired as a screenwriter). For the photography, I sent the rolls to be developed in Sicily; the editing was completed beneath the equatorial sun, in Quito, and the English subtitles were lded in New York and refined in London by a translator and an editor full of madness and passion. I leave the game of the other contaminations to those with the desire to discover them.

For my part, I am grateful for every other instance of direct or indirect assistance that I received, and I continue to believe, like old Charlie, that in the disorder of love any acrobatic feat is possible. And finally, for their acrobatic patience, I also thank everyone who, for various reasons, has had me around them.

It had been my intention to arrange this story musically, to orchestrate it in four movements: allegretto, adagio, andante con variazioni, and finale. And yet I ended up with not much more than a little ballad of upside-down things, which nevertheless kept me company, at dawn, on my own Last Continental Railroad, between Viterbo and Rome. Naturally, life with its sad and joyous events intervened several times to change the direction of the plot and alter the book's tone. For me, this is the last story that I told to a loved one, and it was the occasion of one of his last smiles.

FABIO STASSI, 2013